Leap

leap

JODI LUNDGREN

Second Story Press

Library and Archives Canada Cataloguing in Publication

Lundgren, Jodi, 1966-
Leap / Jodi Lundgren.

ISBN 978-1-897187-85-2

I. Title.

PS8573.U542L43 2011   jC813'.54   C2011-900074-1

"Bedframe" by Graham Lazarovich.
©SOCAN 2002. Used with permission.

Cover photos © Cat London Photography
Edited by Alison Kooistra
Copyedited by Kathryn White
Designed by Melissa Kaita

Printed and bound in Canada

Second Story Press gratefully acknowledges the support of the Ontario Arts Council and the Canada Council for the Arts for our publishing program. We acknowledge the financial support of the Government of Canada through the Book Publishing Industry Development Program.

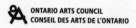

ONTARIO ARTS COUNCIL
CONSEIL DES ARTS DE L'ONTARIO

Canada Council   Conseil des Arts
for the Arts   du Canada

Published by
SECOND STORY PRESS
20 Maud Street, Suite 401
Toronto, ON M5V 2M5
www.secondstorypress.ca

For Geri and Sue

leap

Thursday, June 24th—last day of school!
Sasha and I scored seats high in the bleachers during final assembly. We scanned the crowd, spotting couples and deciding whether or not they'd done it. As the principal droned on, our checklist grew.

Category:	*Tell-Tale Signs:*
a) Haven't done it but hoping to	Sparkly eyes. Frequent laughter at private jokes. Eyelids droop and mouths fall open when the couple touches.
b) Saving it for marriage	Ardent hand-holding. Lingering pecks on the lips. Issues of *Bride* magazine may sprout from girl's backpack, as wedding likely to happen immediately after graduation.
c) Doing it and loving it	A healthy, happy glow. Appear to have just won gold medal for pairs in figure skating. Hands roam the other's body like it's an extension of their own.

It was my turn to make a call. "Fifth row from the front, two seats from the end. Category C."

Sasha curled her fists into binoculars and peered. "Chelsea and Brian? No way! She's a virgin! She nearly fainted in Sex Ed."

"What happened?"

"It was when that chick from the Sexual Health Clinic came to talk to us. The one with blue hair, who looked about twenty? She told us she was 'pro sex.'" Sasha put "pro sex" in quotes by pulsing the first two fingers of each hand. "So we should feel free to ask her anything."

"Uh-oh."

"Someone said, 'What's the difference between a dildo and a vibrator?'" Sasha choked on a laugh. "Pro-sex lady pulled out one of each and set them down on Chelsea's desk. She was supposed to check them out and report back to the class." Sash couldn't hold back the giggles. "She got beet red and bolted from the room."

I squirmed. When we covered Sex Ed in my Health class, we had the regular teacher, and she used a less *hands-on* approach. But I held my ground about Chelsea. "She probably felt guilty! Look at the way Brian's draping his arm over her. His hand is kind of dripping off her body. Like he owns it."

Sasha narrowed her eyes. "I see what you mean. But look at Chelsea." She consulted the notebook and planted her index finger in the second column. "Where's her *healthy, happy glow?*"

We could only see the back of her head, but even so, she didn't exactly radiate. As we watched, she jerked her head so that we could see her profile, chin tucked, hand blocking her mouth. A nail biter.

"I think we need a new category," Sasha said.

I flipped a page in my notebook and picked up my pen.

Sasha cleared her throat. "D. Doing it to stay together."

I scribbled it down. "Tell-tale signs?"

"Nail biting and darting eyes."

I sucked the end of my pen, choosing words.

Category:
d) Doing it to stay together

Tell-Tale Signs:
Nail biting and darting eyes. Looks weighed down when touched. Most commonly found in insecure girls.

Sasha read the entry aloud. "Hey!" She slapped my leg with the back of her hand. "If people do it to stay together, what about *Staying together to do it?*"

Another teacher took over at the microphone. One by one, students' names boomed from the loudspeakers.

"Ew! Who would *do* that?"

Sasha scanned the auditorium. "What about Rob and Amber?" Rob, a senior who'd repeated a grade, starred at rugby. Amber used to cheerlead before the school axed the team. "They don't even seem to *like* each other."

I nodded. "He rolls his eyes at everything she says." We eavesdropped on the seniors at lunch hour whenever we could.

"And she's always flirting with other guys. It drives him crazy. But not enough to break up with her."

I lifted my pen. "What should we call that?"

Sasha gripped the edge of her bleacher and leaned forward. "What did Mr. Hooey say in Science about Canada geese? How they mate for life but aren't faithful? They engage in …" She closed her eyes.

"Extra-pair activity!"

Sasha sprang back to an upright position. "Bingo!" She peered over my shoulder as I wrote.

Category:	*Tell-Tale Signs:*
e) Staying together to do it	Eyes roll at each other's comments. Extra-pair flirting, followed by flare-ups of jealousy. Mostly found in jocks.

"Perfect!" Sasha said.

"NATALIE FERGUSON!"

My name thundered from the PA system and I froze. How could the authorities bust me from so far away? Had they installed zoom-lens cameras to monitor us during assemblies? The girl on my opposite side elbowed me. "Go up to the stage!"

I fought my way down packed bleachers as the announcer called other names. The principal stood at a table piled with trophies and certificates. He passed them to the students who'd been singled out and shook their hands.

I'd won an award?

What had I accomplished this year? Decent grades, but not top of the class. Outside of PE class, I didn't play sports. I hadn't joined any clubs.

"Ow!"

"Sorry!"

As I waded into the sea of latecomers and grade eights forced to sit cross-legged on the floor, I crushed hands and feet, tank-like. No one watching would have guessed that I belonged to a dance team. *Dance team.* That had to be it, even though it was an out-of-school activity. I rolled my shoulders back and tried to show more poise.

When I reached the podium, the principal's assistant whispered, "Name?" Her reading glasses sat low on her nose, and their chain dangled, jowl-like, by her cheeks.

I whispered back. "Natalie Ferguson."

She consulted her clipboard and jutted her chin towards the wings. When I didn't move, she raised her eyebrows and widened her eyes, then shoved my arm. I stumbled off stage, where a couple of kids were already skulking.

"What's going on?" I asked the guy next to me. The only thing hanging lower than his bangs were his pants. He shrugged and pulled out his Nintendo DS.

A girl wearing black lipstick and a dog collar grimaced and shook her head. "We're probably getting the Underachievers' Badge of Shame."

We did form an ill-assorted clump, unlike the proud row of award-winners who spanned center stage, displaying their certificates. The boy standing closest to the wing, seemingly no bigger than a fire hydrant, had won first place in Grade 8 Math. He caught me staring and gave me a superior (if miniature) grin.

The principal's assistant breezed past us and grabbed a vase of flowers off a table. She thrust it into my hands. "The principal is turning sixty-five today."

The kid with the DS perked up. "Does that mean he's going to retire?"

The assistant's face kind of puckered. "Yes, Lewis, you'll be able to start over with a clean slate next year. Give that to me."

She pocketed the console. The goth girl snickered.

"That goes for you too, Danielle."

Fortunately, this lady wasn't on a first name basis with *me*. Until today, that is.

"Natalie, you, Danielle, and Lewis all share Mr. Harbinger's birthday, so when you hear me announce it, go out there and give him these flowers. Everyone is going to sing."

Unbelievable. I was supposed to be spared birthday attention this year while my friends counted down to three o'clock and summer. The principal *would* have to hit retirement age. Not that it came as a shock. With his white hair and raisin-like complexion, he looked about eighty.

Ms. Pucker-Face approached the podium and tapped the mic. "Today is a very special day," she began.

Like it or not, we had to make an entrance, so I tried to corral my fellow birthday boy and girl into some kind of formation. It posed the biggest choreographic challenge of my life. The armful of lilies and gladiolas blocked my view, and the pollen made my eyes water.

"Mr. Harbinger took his teacher training in the 1960s and first worked in our school during his practicum. His classroom was opposite the Home Economics room, and the girls served him up many tasty meals—obviously trying to impress this handsome young teacher." The other staff on stage tittered at that. Beyond lame. "Then in 1968 ..."

I tugged on the other birthday people's sleeves and ducked my head towards the floor. With my toe, I sketched a triangle to show where each of us should stand. They looked confused and slightly hostile, and my eyes itched. I gave up. I tucked the bouquet under one arm and, with my free hand, dug my knuckle into one eyelid, then the other.

"Mr. Harbinger turns sixty-five today. After a lifetime of selfless service as a math teacher, soccer coach, rehearsal director, and principal, he is heading for a richly deserved retirement."

I dropped my hand from my eyes. The principal was exactly half a century older than me, ending his career before mine even started. What was *I* going to do with the next fifty years? The unknown yawned before me with no suspension bridge in sight. I stared into space, unblinking.

A sharp nudge broke my trance. Silence boomed. Her speech finished, Ms. P-F was twisting towards our wing and grinning desperately. I struck out on my own, and she turned back to the mic. "Three of our students are also celebrating birthdays today, and they've graciously agreed to present Mr. Harbinger with a token of our appreciation."

With teary eyes, the principal accepted the flowers. "That speech got to you too, I see. Thank you, dear." My eyelids had practically swollen shut. I could have killed for an antihistamine.

At the sound of applause, I tipped forward to bow, out of habit. But this wasn't a dance performance, and I squeezed my legs together to stop myself. It probably looked like I had to pee. A snort of laughter made me turn to see that my fellow birthday girl and boy had trailed behind, after all.

When the clapping died down, the whole assembly broke into "Happy Birthday." I have to admit, it was touching. Even the goth girl twitched her spooky lips in a kind of smile. As the mass choir roared, Mr. Harbinger and the three of us scrunched together, shoulder to shoulder. What would Sasha have to say about the whole scene? Something cutting and funny, no doubt. I searched the bleachers but couldn't see her anywhere.

Friday, June 25th

Sasha invited me for a swim at her town house today, just the two of us. At first, I couldn't believe my luck. The sun was shining and, for once, we didn't have to share the complex's outdoor pool with Sasha's neighbors. We lathered on sunscreen and stretched out on our towels. Ripples slapped the pool's rim and, in the distance, traffic buzzed. Sash and I see each other almost every day at school or the dance studio, but nothing beats one-on-one time. I was looking forward to a quiet afternoon of tanning and gossip.

"I like your bathing suit," I said. She wore a red velvet bikini that set off her dark hair. "It reminds me of the curtain at the McPherson Playhouse."

"I know! That's why I bought it."

Muffled squeals sounded in the change room. As I eyed the door, it burst open and three other girls from dance team stampeded out. Before I could react, they surrounded my towel and smashed water balloons on the deck. I jumped as water and bits of rubber spattered me. They all shouted, "Happy Birthday!"

"Belated birthday, that is," Claire said. She swiveled to look at the pool, and her blonde ponytail whipped her neck. "We were going to dunk you, but we figured you suffered enough yesterday."

Jamie grumbled and crossed her arms. Not many dancers chose to bulk up as much as she did. If she owned a car, the bumper sticker would say *I'd rather be pumping iron.* "I still think we should dunk her."

Lisa tousled Jamie's hair. "Down, girl!"

Sasha darted a glance at me—neither of us could get away with teasing Jamie like that. But everyone respected Lisa, our unofficial team captain. Jamie sighed and snapped her towel to spread it out. We all settled down to sunbathe.

Lisa lay closest to me in a blue halter-top bikini with boxy bottoms, Marilyn Monroe style. Her knees were bent into triangles and her skin already gleamed a smooth golden color. A twelfth-grader, she didn't usually spend time with us outside the studio. I let my head loll in her direction. "I'm glad you came."

She shaded her eyes and looked at me. "Me too."

"I wish you were taking the summer school this year."

"Thanks for reminding me." She sat up. "Hey, everyone—I've got news. My parents decided to pay for the summer school as a graduation gift. I get to dance with all you lovely people one last time!"

Three cheers and one groan met Lisa's announcement.

"Claire? What the hell? Was that you?" I said.

Claire lay next to Lisa, looking like an Olympic diver in her sporty one-piece. Every year, coaches try to recruit her for the soccer and basketball teams, but she has always chosen to dance instead. She hid her face in her hands. "I didn't want to tell you now and spoil the party. But … I'm not doing the summer school this year."

We all turned to her. "Why not?"

She uncovered her face and let her arms flop wide. "I got a job at The Ice Cream Place. When I'm not working, I just want to swim, camp, bike, and play volleyball on the beach."

No one said anything.

"We'll still see each other! You can come by the store anytime."

"It won't be the same." I pulled at a frayed thread on my towel. *Why do things always have to change?*

"Lighten up," Jamie said. "It's only dance team."

Sasha cleared her throat. "I don't know about you guys, but I'm still recovering from the show. How 'bout we trade massages?"

"Great idea," Lisa said. "Cramming for finals put a few kinks in my neck, too."

We formed a circle like a seated conga line. Behind me, Sasha found knots of spasmed muscle I wasn't even aware of. When she pressed, the pain stabbed. After a while, it dulled, and the tension in my shoulders, neck, and back eased off.

Jamie wriggled in front of me. She was wearing a tank top—or, *muscle shirt* as she likes to call them—and shorts. She spends her share of time in leotards and tights, but outside the studio, she shuns "girly" clothes, even bathing suits. I was kneading her neck with delicate, circular motions of my fingertips. "More pressure!" She slapped her hands on top of mine and flattened them. In partnering class, she digs in too hard and leaves finger-shaped bruises. Apparently, she likes the same technique in a massage. Poor Claire: she ended up in front of Jamie.

During our massage session (coincidence? I think not!), Sasha's older brother sauntered down to the pool and smirked at us. I remember him best as the skinny, pimply thirteen-year-old who would dangle a rubber rat over our shoulders when Sasha and I were trying to do homework, but he has filled out into a buff guy with curly black hair, five-o'clock shadow, and just the right amount of chest hair. He wears a plain silver chain around his neck, and he's always chewing something—gum or a piece of grass or a toothpick. Today, he was drinking a glass of lemonade and crushing ice cubes between his teeth. "How old are you now, Natalie?"

"Fifteen."

"Sweet fifteen and never been kissed!" Jamie offered.

Kevin laughed, but only with his eyes. "I'll bet she's n
innocent as she looks."

"*Na*-ta-lie *Fer*-gu-son *has*-n't been *kissed!*" Sasha said.

Someone always had to revive the limerick issue. In Grade
8, my English teacher pointed out that my name had perfect
dactylic rhythm, which means it sounds like a waltz: *one*-two-
three, *one*-two-three, *Na*-ta-lie *Fer*-gu-son. She instructed the
whole class to make up rhymes about me. (Technically, they were
reverse limericks, as if that helped.) I've never lived it down.

Claire chimed in. "*Went* to the *doc*-tor to *see* what she'd
missed."

After a long pause, during which I hoped they would give
up, Kevin pitched in.

"*Lie* down right *here*, I'll *breathe* in your *ear.*"

Jamie wrapped up (with great originality): "*Na*-ta-lie *Fer*-
gu-son *has*-n't been *kissed!*"

There should really be a law against parents humiliating their
children with weird names, though I realize that my own case
pales against someone like Moon Unit Zappa or Lourdes Leon.

I flipped onto my stomach, head turned away from them.
This position only drew more attention to my biker's thighs and
chunky calves. (Why can't I have long, slender legs like most
dancers?) To make matters worse, my bathing suit was crawling
up my bum. I kept pulling at the elastic, but it's too small for me
this year. Guys get to swim in their shorts; why do girls have to
expose themselves like this? I'd just decided to sit up and wrap
the towel around my waist when Kevin passed by on his way
back inside. I swear he murmured something under his breath.
It sounded like, "Wanna play doctor?"

Did I hear him right?! After his contribution to the limerick, it certainly *sounded* like a come-on.

I watched him lope back to the town house. His spine bisected his long, bare back and arched gently before it disappeared into the khaki shorts that hung loose from his hip bones. I forced myself to flip towards the other girls in case he looked back and caught me gawking.

What is wrong with me? Kevin is off-limits! I don't just mean his age—nineteen, a grown man—but what he did to Sasha. Two summers ago, when I was visiting my dad in Ontario, Sasha made friends with one of her neighbors, a girl named Gina. For a few weeks, they spent all their time together. Gina was trendy, confident, and older—somewhere in between Sasha's age and Kevin's. Sasha practically idolized her, as she let me know in the late-night e-mails she wrote after Gina had gone home.

Then Gina ditched Sasha and began a hot affair with Kevin.

According to Sasha, Kevin moved in on Gina specifically to spite his sister. He had fallen out with his own friends, and he couldn't stand to see Sasha happy when he was lonely. He just had to steal her friend. Furious, Sasha refused to speak to either of them for the rest of the summer. After I got back from Toronto, she practically moved in with us. She didn't even say good-bye when Gina's family left the town house complex in the fall.

Sasha has never forgiven Kevin for the Gina Incident. Since then, the slightest interaction between him and any of her friends upsets her. I don't mention him at all in case she thinks I'm interested and plotting to betray her.

I just hope he doesn't hang around too much this summer. He is getting harder to ignore.

Saturday, June 26th

How I ended up at the public library's annual book purge, I mean sale, on the first Saturday of summer vacation still baffles me. The last thing I remember, I was daydreaming about Kevin in the back seat of Mom's green Volvo, otherwise known as Kermit. (I'd given up the front seat to Paige so I could tune out.) As Mom cranked the steering wheel, all I heard was, "—just stop in for a minute."

You might think that on the first day of her own vacation, a teacher would find something better to do than head for the public building that most resembles a school and surround herself with old, musty books. But you would be wrong. Table after table, both inside and out, overflowed with the dog-eared items. They'd traveled into beds, onto the backs of toilets, and under the edges of plates, to be water-marked and food-stained. Their plastic jackets were cracked and peeling, and their sides were stamped in red: *Greater Victoria Public Library*. Like tattooed convicts, they could leave the prison, but they would never really escape their past.

Mom plundered each table with zest. She picked up a book, flipped it over to scan the back, opened the front cover to read the flap, then leafed through the middle. Sometimes she set the book back down, but with alarming regularity she tucked it under her arm instead. I found a bench by the outdoor tables and settled in with *Monday Magazine* to wait out Mom's scavenger hunt. Once, when I glanced up, Mom was chatting with another woman and waving her free arm around. As if she sensed my eyes on her, she spun around and beelined for me.

"Will you do me a favor and keep an eye on these books so I can keep looking?"

I made sure I sighed loud enough for her to hear. "If I have to."

"Thanks. I won't be long." She fumbled in the pockets of her cardigan and pulled out a barrette. She smoothed her hair back and clipped it into place. "Does that look okay?"

Her fuzzy hair did look better off her face. Tidier, anyway. "Sure." I dropped my eyes to the paper again.

"Natalie?"

I snapped a page to turn it without looking up. "Mm?"

"Can you keep an eye on your sister, as well?"

I rolled my eyes, and Mom dove back into the fray. In a bright orange baseball cap, Paige was easy to keep track of. She was browsing in the children's section. At the age of ten, she still looks up to Mom and tries to copy her. I couldn't help thinking that she was going to find this experience a little more disappointing than most, but pretty soon she came over to stash her finds with me, like Mom had.

"Look at this one about girls in sports."

The oversized encyclopedia featured a hockey goalie on the front, completely hidden behind face cage and body padding. The only way you could tell it was a girl was by the ponytail.

"Don't you think it's cool?"

"I guess so."

My lack of enthusiasm didn't escape my sister.

"You're a spoilsport. Ha, *spoil sport*, get it?"

I mock punched her and she sparred in front of me, bouncing from one foot to the other, her arms tucked in, fists below her chin. Every so often she tilted her body horizontally and shot out her leg. I jumped up and mirrored her moves.

Paige shouted. "Look out!"

It was too late. An old lady had walked up behind me and

my foot made contact with her ribs. I barely grazed her, but she dropped her books, shrieked, and stood there trembling. Mom heard the racket and rushed over just as a library clerk arrived to guide the shell-shocked woman to the bench I'd been sitting on. I picked up the lady's books and apologized, but the clerk waved us back. Mom and Paige gathered their books and headed for the cashier. I waited at a distance from my victim, hoping she would recover and forgive me. I didn't dare to approach again.

"I'm sure it's not serious," someone said.

I started. It was the woman Mom had been talking to. "I saw the whole thing happen. You just gave her a scare." Broad shouldered, she had the solid, reassuring air of a police officer, or a nurse. Her collared shirt could have been a uniform—except for the multicolored circles and lines that decorated it. "You must be Denise's daughter."

I nodded. "Natalie."

"I'm Marine. I met your mom at a creativity workshop for teachers."

"Oh."

I looked past her. Mom and Paige were returning from the cash register. They headed for the lady on the bench.

"Your Mom has a lot of hidden talent."

I wrenched my attention back to this woman who seemed bent on conversation. Her name did sound kind of familiar. "Were you leading the workshop?"

"Yes, that was me."

The details clicked. Mom had raved about Marine's workshop on freeing the artist within. She'd inspired the teachers to finger-paint like kindergartners. "So you teach art?" *Or should I say, Flakiness 101?*

"That's right."

Mom and Paige had stopped at the bench and were speaking to the lady I'd kicked. She lifted up her hands as if she was about to play the piano and shook her head. As soon as Mom came within earshot, I asked, "Is she all right?"

"She'll be fine," Mom said. "Marine …" Her voice turned kind of syrupy to disguise how upset she was with me. "You've met Natalie?"

"Yes. I was just saying I could tell it wasn't serious, right from the get-go."

"Right from the get-go, huh?" Mom chuckled. She herself is always using dorky, old-fashioned expressions like "get-go." Maybe she and Marine speak the same language. "This is my younger daughter, Paige."

"I found an encyclopedia of girls in sports," Paige said.

"How wonderful!" Marine said.

Paige shot me a look to say, *I told you so.*

"I'm doing a softball camp this summer," Paige added.

Hands in her shorts pockets, Marine rocked back on her heels. "I love softball!"

"You should come see me play!" Paige said. "Can she, Mom?"

Mom put her hand on Paige's shoulder and tucked her chin to her neck in embarrassment.

Marine said, "I'd love to!" just as Mom said, "We'll have to see about that."

There was an awkward silence.

"We'd better get going," Mom said. She dropped her hand from Paige's shoulder.

"Sure," Marine said. "Nice to see you."

Mom watched as Marine headed back to the book tables.

Mom could barely tear herself away from the sale, even though her purchases were already weighing her down. When we finally started for the car, she blurted, "Honestly, Nat, I know you wanted to leave, but that was ridiculous."

"It was an accident."

"You were kickboxing in a library!"

"We were outside! Paige started it!"

"Natalie kicked an old lady, Natalie kicked an old lady," Paige sang.

"Paige, that's enough," Mom said.

Paige fell behind Mom and continued to lip-sync the taunt at me. I stuck out my tongue. The problem with having a ten-year-old sister is that sometimes you act like you're ten. "Anyway, it serves you right for forcing me to go to that stupid book sale."

Mom halted, her recycled plastic bags full of books swinging at her sides. "I *beg* your pardon?"

I looked at the ground and pursed my lips. I didn't want to take it back. I tried to keep walking.

"Natalie, I'm waiting."

I waited too. A couple of people passed by and Mom didn't start up again until they were out of earshot.

"If you're sick of tagging along on shopping trips with me, we can go right back to the mall and return those clothes I just paid for. And if you want to be so independent, you're welcome to get a summer job. I'm sure your father can get a refund for the dance intensive."

Her words made me blush. "I'm sorry." No reaction. "I'm *sorry*, okay?"

We loaded into Kermit in silence. If this keeps up, it's going to be a very long summer.

Sunday, June 27th

"Forgot" to call Dad today. My excuse: Paige went to a birthday party, which disrupted our joint-call routine. The truth: I wanted to know if *he* would call *me*. Was there really any doubt? Of course he didn't. What else would you expect from a man who has never said "I love you" to his own daughters?

When Dad moved away, he had this image of himself as a heroic warrior going off on a solo quest or some crap like that. Paige and I were like, "Hellooo! We're your *offspring*, remember us?" That's when Mom dove into gender studies. She started quoting fun facts like, "Men are genetically programmed to 'sow their seed' and move on." Not much of what she said was any help.

The truth was, our family never really stood a chance. Mom grew up on the Island, in Courtenay, and couldn't imagine living anywhere else. Dad moved to BC only for university. He hadn't planned to stay. He dreamed of developing software in Toronto; instead, he married Mom and worked as a computer tech. No wonder he decided the marriage was holding him back, that he had to leave to pursue his "bliss." An idea he got from a book by Joseph Campbell. (How ironic that Mom gave it to him in the first place.) I've hated the word *bliss* ever since.

I used to send handwritten letters to Dad when he first moved back to Ontario. I would cut out comics from the newspaper and stuff them into the envelope. Once, Paige followed my example by cutting out a snowman from her favorite picture book. It must have made her think of Dad in the Ontario snow. She mailed it to him and kept the whole thing a secret until the next time I read her the book. When I turned a page, I found the snowman-shaped hole and asked what had happened to him. As she told me, I traced the hole with my finger and willed myself not to cry.

Dad almost never wrote back. After a while I stopped sending him letters and cut-outs, but I still wrote to him in my head.

Dear Dad,
I don't like my teacher. He throws chalk at people when they talk in class. The boy behind me talks all the time. Today I got hit by the chalk. It's so unfair. I bet the teachers in Toronto aren't so mean.

It didn't matter that these imaginary conversations were one-way. Later, I would tell my friends, "My dad says teachers aren't allowed to throw chalk at kids in Ontario. My dad says Mr. Howe would get fired." Sometimes Dad really would give me useful information, but most of the time, *My dad says* and *In Ontario* were openings that let me reinvent the world.

During our real-life conversations every Sunday, I stood in the kitchen with the phone to my ear. It wasn't cordless. Sometimes I wanted a pair of socks, or a drink, but I wouldn't have set down the phone if a hurricane hit.

Monday, June 28th
Sasha and I spent the afternoon at Willows Beach. We sunbathed, sipped iced tea, scoped guys, skimmed magazines, watched volleyball, and generally tried to impersonate California beach bunnies. Finally, Sasha said, "Kill me now, before I die of boredom."

"To hell with this! Let's ride a log like we used to do."

We packed up our bags and stuffed them into a coin-operated

locker near the washroom. I spotted a good-sized log not too far from the water's edge, and we ran to claim it. It was too flat to roll easily, but fortunately not very heavy, so we flipped it over and over until it was floating in the shallow water. Sasha held the "canoe" while I searched for two sticks to serve as paddles or poles. We straddled the log and cast off.

Staying upright took a lot of effort, and every so often, we lost our balance and rolled into bone-piercing cold. Our screeches drew some attention from the guys we had been ogling earlier. But we ignored their hollers, determined to make it to the end of the beach. We docked at the rock islands and picked our way across them into shallower water and then to shore. Below the waist, we'd gone numb, and bits of kelly green seaweed clung to our legs. Sasha walked stiffly, arms stretched out like Frankenstein, and joked that she was Greta the Sea Monster returned from the deep. I copied her walk and pretended to chase her, running on straight legs. We buckled over laughing and raced each other back to the lockers.

As we retrieved our bags, Sasha's stomach growled.

I laughed. "Fish and chips?"

"You're a mind reader."

"Can I use your phone?"

Sasha rifled in her bag and passed me her cell. Mom didn't pick up, but I left a message telling her not to expect me for dinner. When I handed the phone back to Sasha, she flipped it shut and pocketed it.

"Aren't you going to call home?"

She shrugged. "What for?" She unlocked her bike and sped away. I had to pedal hard to catch up.

We ate a greasy, delicious dinner at an outdoor table lit by reddish, horizontal evening light. Our silhouettes stretched all the way across the street. We butted giant heads and lifted shadow fries with massive hands.

Afterwards, we rode towards Sasha's place. She said something over her shoulder that I couldn't hear, then pulled over. "Why are you coming this way?" Her bluntness rattled me.

"I thought I would go with you as far as your place, and carry on from there. It's really not out of my way."

She resumed pedaling at high speed, as if trying to lose me. At her driveway, she stepped off her bike. "So long, then."

My bladder was bursting. I had to ask if I could use the washroom.

"Why didn't you go at the fish and chips shop?" She sighed. "Just let yourself in and use the downstairs one. I'll wait here with your bike."

I shucked off my pack and hurried into the town house.

In the bathroom mirror, I didn't quite recognize myself. My skin tone had deepened, and my hair gleamed with new blonde highlights. I was wearing a bikini bathing suit top, and, in the cool evening air, the outline of my nipples poked through it. My cut-offs, still damp, hugged my hips. Two muscle lines defined my abdomen. Since my legs didn't show in the mirror, I actually looked all right. Even sexy.

A deep male voice rumbled upstairs. I couldn't hear the words, but the tone was angry. It must have been Mr. Varkosky. A high-pitched voice responded. I heard, "None of your business! …"—"the *last time*" … —"you *always* say." A chair was scraped back and a few banging noises followed. I decided not to flush the toilet and slipped into the hallway. Footsteps pounded down the stairs, and Kevin swung around the banister to face me. He stilled himself instantly. His eyes flicked up and down my body a couple of times, then locked on mine. I couldn't look away. After a few seconds, he brought his finger to his lips in a "Shh" sign, winked, and passed me.

My legs trembled and for a second I thought my knees were going to give out. I took a deep breath and rushed back outside.

"What took you so long?" Sasha thrust handlebars at me. "Did anything happen?"

"No." I grabbed my T-shirt out of my pack and pulled it on. "I didn't even flush, for Pete's sake. Chill out."

I pumped my legs to build up speed for the ride home. As I cycled out of the neighborhood, the scene at the Varkoskys' looped in my head. The raised voices upstairs reminded me of our house in the weeks before Dad moved out, when the tension gave me a chronic stomachache. A steep incline forced me to rise from my seat and drive down on the pedals. I crested the hill, breathing hard.

As I coasted down the other side, I replayed the moment with Kevin in the hallway. Just thinking of it made me blush. It took a rush of evening air to cool my cheeks.

Wednesday, June 30th

When I answered the phone this afternoon, a male voice said, "Hi, Natalie."

"Who is this?"

The voice chuckled, and my heart rate sped up: it was Kevin. Maybe he was going to mention our silent encounter the other night. I let Sasha think no one had seen me; had he told her any different? Or was he going to explain that the fight wasn't what it sounded like?

He asked what I was doing for the summer. He told me he'd been tree-planting up north for most of May and June and was going back in a week. Every detail he let drop thrilled me like a private confession: Sasha never should have tabooed him.

"Do you want to go to the fireworks?"

"What?" In my surprise, it came out as a squeak.

He stifled a laugh. "The fireworks, you know, for Canada Day, down in the Inner Harbour."

He was asking me out. He's *nineteen!* Old enough to drink and go to bars.

Snapping and crunching filled the silence. I guessed he was making short work of a toothpick while he waited for me to recover from my shock.

"I'll have to ask my mom." How stupid did that sound? "I mean, she might need me to babysit Paige."

"All right, you ask your mom." He was mocking me again. Did he realize I'd never dated before? "But hurry, this offer is only good for a limited time."

"Huh?"

"Canada Day is tomorrow."

"Oh." He must think I have the IQ of one of those toothpicks he's always demolishing.

After I hung up, I wanted to phone Sasha so we could dissect the situation like we always do. But a) Kevin might answer and b) I couldn't tell Sasha that Kevin had asked me out: She would hate him for attempting another Gina Incident. Worse, she would hate *me* for even considering the invitation. My heart kept pounding and my neck started to itch.

I locked myself in the bathroom. I faced the mirror, lifted my chin, and fingered my bumpy red rash. *I don't know if I want to go. He always seems to be making fun of me. Does he even like me? Or is he just trying to piss off Sasha? If I go, will she ever forgive me?*

Unlike me, Sasha has dated. Last fall, she had a whole four-week relationship. I barely saw her for the "Month of Colin"—she even skipped dance class. And when she called, which wasn't often, he was the *only* topic of conversation. She could have at least tried to set me up on a double-date with the two of them. It's not like I didn't ask. *So why do I need her approval to date, even if she and Kevin do share DNA?*

Paige knocked on the bathroom door. "Nat, you've been in there forever! I want my water gun."

I opened the door and she ducked under my arm.

"You must be the only ten-year-old who still uses bath toys."

Paige stuck out her tongue and made a farting sound.

I found Mom immersed in one of her library discards on the porch. She was wearing a sundress with an elasticized bust and a wide-brimmed hat. I don't know if she was just trying to get rid of me, but she didn't seem to think it was weird that Kevin would ask me out. She obviously doesn't remember the Gina Incident, which, if you consider how much time Sasha spent at our house venting about it that summer, is kind of disturbing. She said it was all right with her if I went. When I didn't respond, she raised her sunglasses and squinted at me. "Do you *want* to go?"

"I'm not sure."

"Don't you think it would be fun?"

"I don't know."

"Well, don't force yourself into anything you're not comfortable with."

Her glazed expression meant that her book was "unusually engrossing" and that she wasn't going to be much help in working

this through. Why would she be? She hasn't dated since she and
Dad split up six years ago, and at this rate, she never will again.
She binge-reads the way other addicts binge-drink or binge-eat.
I'm never going to be like her.

"Have you ever thought of wearing latex gloves when you're
reading those?"

Mom gave me a blank look. "Hm?"

"Never mind."

She probably thinks it's okay to go out with Kevin because
I'm such good friends with Sasha. But I don't know Kevin that
well; he's always just been Sasha's older brother.

I wonder if Sasha knows that Kevin phoned me?

Maybe he won't even call me back.

Thursday, July 1st / Friday, July 2nd, midnight

Hundreds of us packed the causeway from Laurel Point to the
Inner Harbour and waited for it to get dark. People bobbed in
canoes and outboard motor boats, too. The show didn't start till
after ten o'clock. Kevin and I claimed spots right by the garden that spells *Welcome to Victoria* in begonias and pansies. We
saw the glittering explosions *and* their reflections on the water.
Sometimes the light zoomed right at us, and the crowd gasped
like one person. At the end, "O Canada" played, and red and
white-gold sparks filled the sky.

Kevin smoked the whole time. That must be why he's always
chewing something when he's at home—he's not allowed to
smoke in the town house. He looked amused by the whole cele-
bration, and people usually smiled at him as they passed. I envied
his confidence. When the national anthem played, he sang at the
top of his lungs. Some drunken teenagers stumbled over to join

him, and everyone linked arms, including me. As I swayed back and forth, scrambling to support the wasted girl beside me, it hit me: I was downtown at night without a parent, mine or anyone else's. Freedom smelled of salt water and outboard motor oil.

As we walked back to the car, Kevin told me more about tree-planting, about the blackflies and the rain and working ten-hour days six days in a row, then going in to Prince George and getting drunk on his day off. He noticed me shiver as the wind picked up and put his arm around me. "For warmth," he said. It seemed to me that we got some funny looks; was it because he's so much older than me?

On the way home, he took the "scenic route" and stopped at a pull-off overlooking the ocean. He twisted the keys in the ignition and the car rumbled to a halt. Wind rushed in the window.

"Is this your first date, Natalie?"

I didn't want to answer him. The amused expression that seemed to make everyone else warm up to him didn't feel so good when he trained it on me. He was laughing at me with his eyes.

"Hey, it's okay. Only, maybe you don't know what to expect."

I felt trapped in the car. "I don't know what you mean, but I want to go home."

"Already?" He reached out and smoothed back my hair. I could smell the nicotine on his fingers. The calluses on his palm scraped my cheek, but he touched me gently. It felt okay. "I was so surprised when I saw you downstairs the other night."

"I know, I'm sorry. It's just—"

He shook his head. "No worries. But you want to know what I was thinking?"

His fingers brushed a sensitive spot on the back of my neck. I shuddered.

"I give up."

"What a babe."

In the center of my chest, something strawberry-sized melted into liquid warmth.

"After, I kept picturing you standing there, and that's when I knew I had to call."

He put his arm around my shoulders, pulled me towards him, and squeezed. His hands rubbed my back and razor stubble scratched my face. His mouth slid onto mine. I pressed my lips together but he tongued them open, his jaws wide. Yuck, smoker's breath. He was suddenly breathing hard, like he'd just surfaced from underwater, desperate for air. It scared me. I jerked my head and twisted in his arms. "Let me go!"

"What's the matter?"

I was huddling against the door on my side of the car. He seemed annoyed, but not for long.

"Never done that before, huh?" He winked. "It gets better. Cheer up, I'll take you home."

When he dropped me off, he gave me a light punch in the arm. He didn't say he'd call me. I wished him luck with the blackflies.

Na-ta-lie *Fer*-gu-son *now* has been *kissed.*

Saturday, July 3rd

Mom, Paige, and I were grocery shopping when I spotted a woman weighing a grapefruit in her palm. One look at her coiffed hair—with its subtle gold and copper highlights and its complicated array of angles and flips—and I knew who it was: Mrs. Varkosky, mother of Sasha and Kevin. I tried to steer Mom over to the bulk food bins where she could busy herself scooping trail mix and organic rice. But she frowned and said she wasn't finished in the produce section yet. I squeezed avocadoes absently and willed Mrs. Varkosky not to turn around.

Mrs. V. works as a real estate agent and dresses the part: skirts and blazers that change colors with the seasons, shoes with heels that change height and width with the trends. As Mom would say, she wears war paint and business armor. Mom's own fashion motto is "comfort first." True to form, she was wearing a sack-like dress and wide, flat sandals.

But Mom's outfit wasn't my biggest concern. There was what my mother might *say*. Possible gems: "What do you think of the budding romance between our children?" Ha, wouldn't Mrs. V. freak if she assumed that Sasha and I were gay? Or: "It was very *kind* of your son to take my daughter out on her very first date," like he'd performed an act of charity. Little does she know that Kevin's not in it for the Cub Scout points.

Just then, Mrs. Varkosky looked up and caught me staring. Two vertical lines have etched themselves between her eyebrows. Sasha said she's considering Botox. A weary expression flitted across her face before she smiled.

"*Don't say anything.*" I spoke into Mom's ear without moving my lips.

Mom shot me a startled look and said, "Hello, Pauline."

I found my voice. "Hi, Mrs. Varkosky."

"It's the Ferguson girls. How are you all today? Aren't you grown up, Paige! Lovely performance the other week, Natalie. And how's the exhausted teacher? Enjoying your summer vacation, Denise?"

Luckily, we only had time to murmur brief responses before Mrs. V. had to dash. Paige watched Mrs. V. weave her way through the crowded store to the cash registers. "That lady is nice, but in a mean way," she said.

For the rest of the shopping trip, I was so distracted that even Mom noticed. When she teased me about it, I snapped at her. We didn't talk the whole way home.

Sunday, July 4th

It's settled: Paige is going to Toronto in August on her own. She'll stay with Dad for three weeks, during which he has *promised* to take vacation. Paige always gets the benefit of Mom and Dad's screw-ups with *me*. Last year, Paige and I were all set to visit Dad together, as usual, when she came down with appendicitis and had to have an emergency operation. Naturally, she couldn't go. I hated to leave with her in the hospital. I kept seeing her greenish face dwarfed by the huge, white pillow. Everyone said there was no point in us both missing the trip, and besides, she was doing fine. I traveled alone. For the next two and a half weeks, I languished in Dad's condo in Oakville while he dealt with an "urgent project" that had come up "without his control," even though he had booked the weeks off. I was bored and lonely and to top it all off, the **air-c**onditioner broke.

Dad's girlfriend, Vi, wasn't too pleased about it either. She had scheduled her holidays at the same time as he had and couldn't postpone them. With Dad busy, she made a half-hearted attempt to entertain me. Our first and only shopping trip ground to a halt when I convinced her that, no, my parents didn't give me a clothing allowance. Unable to fathom an adolescent girl who didn't live to shop, Vi fled to her family's cabin in Parry Sound.

At the end of my stay, Dad finally made time for me, and we raced around the city, packing in Science World, the CNE, the

Shakespeare play in High Park, and Sunnyside Beach. He took two rolls of film in three days. Vi must have conveyed her shock about my wardrobe to Dad because he also took me shopping at the Eaton Centre on Yonge Street and bought me so much stuff it wouldn't fit into my suitcase; I had to ship a parcel. When Paige saw the photos and the clothes, she wanted the same chance to hog Dad's attention. So, this year Paige will visit that cabin on Parry Sound with Dad and Vi—they'll canoe and swim and maybe water ski.

I'll just have to make the best of it here. Mom might go to a resort with her friend Marine in August. They'll haul a crate of novels each, I imagine. They'll need a wheelbarrow to move them into the cabin. Mom said Marine invited both of us, but I don't want to be stuck out in the middle of nowhere with not one but two middle-aged bookworms. So I *might* be living here on my own for a week. Maybe Sasha could stay with me. *If* we're still friends, that is.

I wonder if Kevin will call me before he leaves town.

Monday, July 5th

Sasha and Jamie were basking in a lozenge of sunlight on the wooden floor of the dance studio when I arrived for the first day of the summer intensive. Sasha looked at me and darted her eyes away without smiling. She snuck another look at me in the mirror. Had Kevin blabbed to her about the date? Was she already thinking of me as "Gina the Second, Traitor"?

I wanted to approach her, but she wasn't making it easy. She reached for her toes and all I saw was the curve of her back and her hair in its tidy bun. She was wearing a new, eggplant-colored leotard. As I moved closer, Sasha and Jamie burst out laughing.

My intestines shriveled as I watched Sasha's profile and Jamie's face. The two of them have perfect complexions. My nose was starting to shine and my upper lip prickled with sweat.

Thankfully, Ms. Kelly flung open the door to the studio at that moment and strode in. "Good morning, girls! Find a place on the floor. Natalie, don't stand there like a blue heron stalking minnows. There's a spot down front."

I settled in next to the junior girls. Lisa slipped into the studio at the last minute. Outside the window, gravel crunched under the wheels of her boyfriend's blue pickup truck. He used to honk as he pulled away, until Ms. Kelly put a stop to it. As Stretch and Conditioning class began, it occurred to me (for the millionth time) that Ms. Kelly should have been a drill sergeant. She makes us do push-ups and sit-ups, and she yells at the people who slow down, rest, or groan. In the center work, she stands beside each of us with a ruler held level with the tops of our heads and makes us kick it. Anyone who doesn't reach it, she sentences to fifteen minutes of extra hamstring stretches and splits per day. Sometimes she prods us with that ruler—"Pull up your knees! … Turn out from the tops of your thighs!" Poke, poke.

When she choreographs, Ms. Kelly cleans each set of eight counts before she continues. She says that learning the whole piece before starting to clean creates lazy dancers with bad habits. So, in jazz class today, we repeated the first few bars of the piece *ad nauseam*: "Stretch your lines! Are those *hands* on the ends of your arms, or dead fish? Energy in the fingertips! … Point your feet! … Synchronize your movement! Natalie, this is not a solo!"

Sash and I didn't talk all day. She was avoiding me, I think.

Kevin should leave to go tree planting soon. Then things can get back to normal.

Wednesday, July 7th

We thrust our hips from side to side. We rippled our torsos in body waves. We draped our arms over our heads. With our backs to the audience, we put our hands on our hips and turned our heads over our shoulders with a come-hither look. We slid in splits to the floor, leaned back on bent elbows, and fanned our legs.

At the end of jazz class, Ms. Kelly made us try on our costumes for a photo shoot: red Lycra unitards with plunging neck and back lines. We bunched up in a pose, and for a split second, when I looked in the mirror, I couldn't tell which one I was. Then I zeroed in on the legs. I was the one with the thickset, bow-legged calves. Gross. Ms. Kelly circled us, snapping one photo after another. I checked out the rear view. The V-neck exposed a bunch of zits on my back that I didn't even know were there. I can't wear those stupid unitards anymore. I might have to quit dance altogether.

Ms. Kelly let the camera drop from her face and exhaled in exasperation. "Natalie, do you think you could wipe that sneer off your face?"

I flashed her a fake smile. Some of the other girls were goofing off, sticking out their butts and squishing their boobs together to make cleavage.

Ms. Kelly sighed. "I can see it's hopeless to continue. You've obviously shut off your brains for the day. But before you go, I have an important announcement to make."

Jamie and Sasha were bent over, looking through their legs into the mirror. "I can't believe this is supposed to look sexy!" Jamie said, red in the face.

"Jamie and Sasha! May I have your attention, please?"

They whipped themselves upright, and Sasha staggered a

little. "Whoa, head rush." Jamie steadied her with a hand on her back.

"I'm happy to announce that next week, and the week after, you're going to have a guest teacher, Petra Moss. Petra is one of my star graduates, and I want you to show her that our standards remain as high as ever! Understood?"

With mock obedience, we echoed in unison: "Understood."

Petra Moss. Sounds like a bitchy prima donna. She'll probably be just like Ms. Kelly, only younger.

Thursday, July 8th
Kevin called.

"I want to see you before I go, and I leave tomorrow, so what about tonight?"

It was already eight o'clock. "Isn't it too late?"

"When does your mom go to bed?"

"She usually stays up late reading, why?"

"When do you go to bed?"

"Eleven or so." On my bedside table, the clock's second hand jerked forward.

"Could you pretend to go to bed, and then sneak out?"

"What do you mean?"

"Is your bedroom on the ground floor?"

"Yeah, but …"

"Could you climb out the window?"

I moved to the window and pulled my blind shut, even though it was still light out. "What for?"

"I just think it would be fun to see you before I go."

I wanted to say, "Why didn't you call me earlier, then?" but for some reason I couldn't. "What time?"

"How about eleven thirty? I'll meet you at the top of your street." Tick-tock, tick-tock. Why couldn't I have a quiet digital clock like most normal twenty-first century people?

"I don't know if I can."

"Sure you can. I did it all the time when I was your age."

I didn't say anything.

"If you don't want to hang out, I'll have no choice but to call my friends Tyler, Steve, and Brad. I have spent the last four nights in a row with them. All they do is drink, and I do believe my liver is starting to disintegrate."

I took a deep breath. "I'll think about it."

He gasped. "I throw myself at your mercy for the sake of my health, and all you can do is *think* about it?"

I had to laugh. "Sorry."

"No, don't apologize. I respect a girl with principles. Go ahead and think about it. But remember, you only live once."

He crushed some ice between his teeth as he hung up. I tried that the other day and it *hurt*! He must have no sensitivity to hot and cold.

My stomach is fluttering and one leg is pulsing, which makes my whole bed jiggle. I don't know what to do. Sneaking out sounds like an adventure. I might get a second chance at kissing. But, can I trust him? I'm just not sure.

It's a warm night, inviting, almost tropical.

Should I go?

Wee hours

I was just getting ready to attempt escape when Mom tapped on my door. "Natalie?"

Stupid me for leaving my light on. It was 11:20, and I was sitting on the edge of my bed. "What is it?"

Mom seemed to interpret this as "come in." She opened the door. She was wearing her plaid housecoat and slippers. "You're still dressed?"

My second mistake.

"Are you feeling okay?"

"Yeah."

"Aren't you tired from all your dancing?"

"I guess not."

"Why don't you come and play Scrabble, then? I'm not ready for bed yet either."

"Don't you have anything to read?"

"Oh, yes. *Tess of the d'Urbervilles*. It was one of my favorite books when I was your age. I'm rereading it to see why I found it so powerful back then." She pulled off the headband that she uses to keep the hair out of her eyes when she's reading and rubbed her scalp. "But I've just finished Part One, so it's a good time to stop for the night. Besides, my eyes are getting sore."

Figures. The only time she takes an interest in me is when she's too tired to read. Well, bad timing. If only that author had made Part One a little longer. Thanks to him, I couldn't meet Kevin.

"What do you think, Nat? Want to play?"

I sighed. "I guess so."

She brewed chamomile tea as the kitchen clock ticked in the midnight stillness. A crane fly flew in the window and landed on my forearm. When I brushed it off, it wobbled into flight, all spindly legs and feeble wings. Mom made some good words, like *brink* and *quest*. I wonder if Kevin walked by and saw our light. It bothered me to think of him out there, but I felt thankful, after all, that Mom was awake.

Friday, July 9th

"Kevin's mad at you," Sasha said as we changed into our pointe shoes at the back of the studio.

"What do you mean?"

"He says you stood him up."

I crisscrossed long pink ribbons over my ankle and wrapped them around my leg.

"He says he waited at the end of your street for half an hour last night.

I fumbled with the knot, my head bent.

"Is that true, Nat?"

"How should I know?"

"Is it true you were supposed to meet him?"

I couldn't look at her.

"What were you two planning to do, anyway? Go have sex in his car? You know he got a girl pregnant last year, don't you?"

Ms. Kelly called, "Sasha and Natalie, will you be joining us for pointe?"

My skin prickled.

"Coming," Sasha sang.

Ms. Kelly divided the class into two groups for the long combination. During my group's turn, Sasha and Jamie lounged on the barre, whispering and watching me. I could only cope with the *relevés* and *echappés*. After that, I lost my center. I couldn't balance on the *piqués* and couldn't pirouette. Ms. Kelly kept me after class for what seemed like a thousand repetitions.

"My star pupil, Petra Moss, is going to be teaching you ballet next week, and I'd rather you weren't a *total* embarrassment to me," Ms. Kelly said.

When her back was turned, I put my hands on my hips and flapped my lips open and shut: *blah, blah, blah.* I was already sick of hearing about Petra Moss.

By the time I left the studio, everyone was eating lunch on the grass. The seniors were clustered on the far side of the lawn, in the shade of an oak tree. When I approached, they all stopped talking. Someone muttered, "Slut." It must have been Sasha. They all stared at me.

My stomach knotted up. The sun blazed and my toes were bleeding. I did an about-face and returned to the studio. In my mind, I remained with the girls on the grass and watched myself walk. I saw the back of my head, my stiff spine, my lumbering legs, the image overexposed in the bright noon sun. Someone called my name and I ignored it. I entered the building, blinded by the sudden dimness, grabbed my bag, and left.

Mom had dropped me off, so I didn't have my bike. Miles from home, without a plan, I followed the road to the Dallas cliffs. Open ocean. I needed that breeze; I wanted that water to cool my feet. Stairs led down to the beach. I kicked off my shoes. The salt stung the ripped blisters but soothed the swelling. I burrowed in my bag for cucumber slices and apple juice.

Women with young children dotted the beach. On the cliff top, bikers sped past, and a couple of people flew kites. Normal people enjoyed the summer outdoors. They didn't coop themselves up in a studio. I didn't have to go back to that nasty place.

But how could they label me a "slut"?

I eased my feet back into my sandals and climbed the stairs. I wanted to stroll—like a "normal person"—but my blisters hurt too much. I sank into the first available bench and stared at the waves.

"Hey."

Someone sat down beside me. I turned my head. Kevin! He lit a cigarette.

"How did you know I was here?"

"Didn't. This is called bumping into each other."

"Right. Sorry, I'm just not myself today."

"Then who are ya?" He turned his head towards me as he took a drag.

"Well, according to your sister, I'm a slut."

"Get out of here."

"What did you tell her anyway?"

He looked straight ahead, folded his left arm across his chest, and exhaled. "I told her the truth, that you stood me up."

I swiveled and grabbed the backrest with one hand. "I never promised to meet you, I just said I'd try, and now she thinks we were planning to have sex in your car!"

"Uh-oh."

"Yeah, and she said you got some girl pregnant last year."

He slouched and stretched his legs further onto the sidewalk. A dog walker had to alter her course to get around him. Kevin waited for her to pass before he said in a low voice, "Don't believe everything you hear, Natalie."

"It doesn't matter what *I* believe; she's turned the whole studio against me!" My voice caught in my throat. I jumped up and ran down the path. I didn't want to cry in front of him. But he caught up to me and held my arm.

"I'm sorry, Natalie. I shouldn't have said anything to Sash. That was really stupid of me."

I wiped my eyes and stepped away from him. "What are you doing here, anyway? You were supposed to be leaving town."

"Shipment of trees got held up, so the contract got postponed. I'd rather spend the extra days kicking around here than up in Prince George." He flipped his wrist to look at his watch. "You playing hooky this afternoon, or what?"

"I'm not going back there."

"Can I give you a lift somewhere?"

Behind him, the cliff dropped into the sea. A parasurfer caught a gust and flew ten feet into the air. "All right."

We crossed a field, ducking Frisbees, to reach his car. "What do you say we pick up some cold ones and head out to a lake I know?"

I shrugged. If my reputation was ruined, I could at least have my adventure. "Why not?"

He stopped at a Cold Beer and Wine store and disappeared inside. When he returned with a six-pack, my shoulders tightened. What if he drank them all? How would I get home?

We left the city and drove down country roads lined with evergreens that cast cool shadows. Horses grazed in fields. I breathed in the scent of pine and began to relax. I'd forgotten how much I loved the country. Mom and Dad used to take us hiking, but that had pretty much stopped by the time they split up. And Mom's idea of an expedition usually involves a bookstore, not a park.

"It's nice to get out of the city, don't you think?" Kevin said.

We'd been driving in silence. A comfortable one. "Yeah."

Kevin turned down a narrow, tree-lined road and, after a

minute or two, pulled over and cut the engine. "Where are we?" I couldn't see a lake or any other cars.

"We're here. Hop out." Kevin grabbed the beer and led the way down a dirt path to the shore of a lake about the size of two skating rinks. We climbed onto a ramshackle wooden pier. Fir trees surrounded the lake, its surface a calm, green mirror.

He twisted open a beer and passed it to me. I hesitated to pick it up. Then he cracked one for himself and said, "Cheers. To playing hooky."

That got to me: Why shouldn't I play hooky once in a while? I'm not getting any rewards for being a "good girl" anyway, not the way my so-called friends treated me today. I took a swig.

I'd tried beer before, with Sasha. It isn't my favorite thing. But it went down smoothly on such a hot day. Soon we were drinking a second. I felt even more floaty than I had when I'd left the studio. The blisters on my toes throbbed every time my heart beat.

"Time for a dip!" Kevin said.

He stripped to his shorts and jumped in. With my leotard for a swimsuit, I followed him. The cool water buoyed me as I floated on my back. Treetops pointed into the dome of blue sky. I sculled with my hands and feet. When I tried to stand up and couldn't find bottom, I panicked and thrashed. That sobered me up. I swam back to the pier and climbed out.

"Getting out so soon?"

"What are you trying to do, drown me? Bringing me out here, giving me beer, telling me to swim?" Black spots swarmed my vision.

As Kevin pulled himself out of the water, his muscles flexed and water ran off his arms and chest. He shook his bangs from his eyes and squatted beside me. "Are you okay? I forgot you're not used to drinking. Two beer is probably quite a lot for you." He rubbed my shoulder. "Are you okay?"

The spots had cleared. "Yeah." I lay down, the wooden slats under my back, and he lay beside me on his stomach. He closed his eyes and, to my surprise, started to snore. I turned my head as he slept. His wet curls glistened. Around his neck, his silver chain caught the light. He had folded his arms under his head and his biceps rippled a bit. I reached out and stroked his arm.

He opened his eyes, startled. Then he grinned at me. He slid his palm on to my stomach. Heat spread like tiger balm below his hand, making my thighs and crotch tingle. I twisted onto my side. He faced me, too, then we were kissing, blood rushing in my ears, our bare skin touching, still cool from the lake. His tongue tasted like beer this time, not cigarettes. A much better flavor. He nuzzled my neck and moved his head down my chest. He pulled down my top so I was naked to the waist, then smothered me with his body—it was too much, too much, I liked it but not so fast, the nerve endings died in my breasts, they were lumps of fat jiggling on my ribs with no sensation as he gnawed them and tossed his head like a dog with a rubber toy.

We heard voices, thank God, and that made him stop. He threw his towel across me and rolled away. Otherwise ... I hate to think what might have happened. I lay on the dock taking deep breaths and fumbling with my leotard. When I made it home, I told Mom I was sick and escaped to my room. Dizzy with sunstroke and beer and kisses. An underage drinker and worse. And none of this would have happened if Sasha hadn't called me a slut.

Saturday, July 10th

How to erase yourself: lie on a chaise longue and cover your face with a baseball cap. Keep a pitcher of iced tea beside you and balance a glass on your sternum. Drink from a bendable straw. Don't move. Don't talk. Don't obsess. (Forget about that guy's mouth on your neck, his hand on your leg, his weight on your chest …)

"Let's sleep under the stars tonight!" Paige said.

I groaned.

"What's the matter? Don't you think it would be fun?"

I didn't bother to move the cap. It had built-in ventilation holes but still smelled like sweated-in canvas. "I just can't get excited about anything today."

"Fine." Paige hates teenage apathy. "I'll call Jessica." She stamped inside.

But Jessica can't make it, so it's back to me. I wish I didn't feel so low. I've taken two baths and brushed my teeth five times, but it's like washing a window that won't get clean. Fingerprints stay smudged on the wrong side of the glass.

Night

"Cassiopeia is supposed to be a woman tied to a chair," Paige said. She learned constellations on a rainy day at her softball camp last week.

"Really?" I studied the pinpricks of light overhead. "It just looks like a *W* to me."

We lay side by side in our sleeping bags on the balcony over the garage. The smell of resin wafted from a pair of fir trees that brushed the house. I breathed it in deep.

"It was her punishment for bragging about her and her daughter and how beautiful they were."

"I can't imagine Mom bragging about us, can you?"

Paige thought about it. "I guess not." She paused. "I'm sure she's proud of us, though." Her statement hung in the air. "Aren't you?"

I had to struggle not to poison Paige's view of our parents with my own doubts. "I'm sure she's proud of *you*, Paige."

Stargazing made my problems shrink, anyway: I was just one miniscule life form in an infinite cosmos. Every time I exhaled, the night air absorbed a little of my worry and left behind sweet fatigue. We spotted the Big Dipper, the Little Dipper, and the North Star. Paige claimed to see a constellation called Lyra. *That would make a pretty name for a girl,* I thought, as I drifted further along the Milky Way.

When I woke up in the middle of the night, the stars had swept into different positions. It made me dizzy to think of the earth moving that fast underneath them. Next month, the meteor shower happens, and I wish Paige was staying so we could watch it. Or better yet, that I was going to Ontario with her. Maybe I can still get Dad to change his mind.

Sunday, July 11th

Mom, Paige, and I picnicked at Thetis Lake today. Mom regaled us with the plot of *Tess of the d'Urbervilles,* which she just finished re-reading. It was a bit much for Paige, and she went off to get a Popsicle at the concession stand. Mom was worked up about the way Tess's fiancé treats her once he discovers that she had a child without being married: as a used, impure woman. And even worse, Mom says that Tess only gets pregnant after being raped! Mom was really angry about the whole situation. She wasn't blaming the author; she says he was exposing the "hypocrisy and sexism in Victorian society." (I think I'm quoting her right.)

My gross feeling lifted as she talked about it. For a few

moments, nothing that happened this week mattered. Everything shifted perspective. That's the thing about Mom. She's so clueless that I could never tell her about fooling around with Kevin, or being called a slut, but sometimes she creates these mental viewpoints that give me a new way of seeing things. I dove into the clear green lake and swam to Goose Island—which was, as always, carpeted with turds.

Monday July 12th

As I approached the change room this morning, raised voices inside made me pause with my hand on the doorknob. Tension pushed Sasha's voice up half an octave. I heard Kevin's name and yanked open the door. Sasha had her back to me and was pulling on bike shorts, which Ms. Kelly allows instead of tights in hot weather. She spun around when she heard me and snapped her mouth shut. Jamie, never the most sensitive person, bulldozed ahead. "So what happens now? Will he go to jail?"

I couldn't hold back. "What happened?"

Jamie said, "Kevin was driving under the influence and he got into an accident."

"Oh my God!" *How much of that beer did he drink at the lake?*

"I'm not discussing this with her." Sasha turned her back to me and rummaged in her knapsack.

Jamie glanced from Sasha to me and back. She looked almost smug, which confirmed my suspicion that she'd always resented our friendship. I waited to see whose side she would take, but I should have known. Jamie stepped up to Sasha, slipped one arm around her shoulders, and murmured words I couldn't make out—she was either building Sasha up or tearing me down, maybe both at once. Either way, my presence obviously grated

on them. I bolted and, as I flung open the outside door, crashed
into Lisa.

"What's wrong?" she said.

"Sasha's brother got into an accident and she won't talk to
me. I've got to get out of here."

She touched my arm. "Wait—I'll come with you. I heard
Kevin's okay."

Lisa guided me to Con Brio, a café on a corner a few blocks
from the studio. It has two walls of windows, counters filled with
newspapers and magazines, and long wooden tables where you
can play chess or backgammon. I'd never been in. Sitting in cafés
was for grown-ups.

Grown-ups. Luckily, I didn't say that out loud. Older people,
I meant. We crossed the threshold and entered the shop. Lisa—
who *is* older, after all—ordered two iced lattes and chose a table
for two in the window. The sun at her back made her dark hair
glow with auburn highlights. She pushed one of the tall glasses
across the table to me. We faced each other, stirring in sugar.

"I'll tell you what I know," Lisa said. She didn't use the
excited tone that Sasha reserves for juicy gossip. She was matter-
of-fact. Her boyfriend and Kevin have friends in common, soccer
players. They'd held an after-game party on Friday night. "The
accident happened on his way home. He ran a red light and got
sideswiped." Lisa twisted her glass in her hands. The barista was
hammering at the espresso machine.

Kevin didn't sustain serious injuries, but his license was suspended. He has to go to court and will miss the second half of
tree-planting season. "His parents are so angry that they want
him out of their place, like, yesterday."

I stared at the tabletop.

Lisa touched my hand. "It could have been a lot worse. And I've seen other guys smarten up after an accident like that. In the meantime, I wouldn't take anything Sasha says too personally." I frowned at my glass and poked at the ice cubes with my stir stick. "Did you hear her call me a slut when I walked up to you guys at lunch on Friday?"

The roaring of the espresso machine drowned out Lisa's response. A young woman struggled to push a stroller into the café until a man entering behind her held the door. I chewed my lip and waited for the grinding, hissing, and banging to cease.

"No, I didn't," Lisa said.

"I'm sure I heard her say it, and then I figured you'd all been talking about me."

"I wouldn't have joined in that kind of gossip, Natalie." The warmth in Lisa's face convinced me. Sasha may have her issues with me—maybe she even hates me right now—but that doesn't mean everyone at the studio sides with her. "How's your latte?"

I'd forgotten to try it. I took a sip: It tasted way more like a milkshake than I was expecting. "Delicious." Being a grown-up might not be so bad.

Before I knew it, I was telling Lisa about seeing the fireworks with Kevin, the phone call asking me to sneak out, the trip to the lake—and the pain of having to keep it all from Sasha because of the Gina Incident.

No one had ever listened to me like Lisa. She radiated compassion like a heat lamp. It made me dissolve. My torso jerked and tears streamed down my face, warm and wet. I can't remember the last time I cried in front of someone. I let my hair fall forward to hide my face.

I wanted to ask Lisa so much more—was she having sex

with her boyfriend, Luke? Had he pressured her into it, or did she really want to? When they were making out, did her skin ever feel numb, like it belonged to somebody else?

On second thought, there was no way Lisa was a "Doing it to stay together" sort of girl. I grinned at her and wiped my eyes with the back of my hand.

"Feeling better?"

"A little."

"Why don't you rinse off your face, and we'll head back for ballet?"

As we approached the studio, Lisa grabbed my hand. "*Merde.*"

"Hm?"

"That means 'good luck.' Dancers say it to each other before going on stage." She chuckled. "But really, it's French for *shit.*"

Recorded piano music was drifting out the window. We were late for class.

"Then *merde* to you, too." I returned Lisa's hand squeeze. "We'll need luck, 'cause we're in shit."

We slipped into the studio when Ms. Kelly's back was turned. Without even turning around, she snapped, "Have you girls decided to grace us with your presence? How lucky we are!" Some of Lisa's strength must have rubbed off on me because Ms. Kelly didn't really get to me. I just took a deep breath and sucked in my belly.

At lunch, Sasha and Jamie left and didn't return for the afternoon. The way everyone keeps skipping classes, Ms. Kelly must think it's mutiny. She'll probably sit us all down for a lecture tomorrow.

Tuesday, July 13th

She walked into the studio like she was riding on wind. Her pants, cropped at the shin, billowed around her legs as she moved. Her torso bloomed out of her waist and branched into long, expressive arms. "Hello girls, my name is Petra. Welcome to Advanced Ballet. We'll start in the center." Her voice rang with silvery tones: church bells, waterfalls.

We raised our eyebrows at each other, and not only because of her voice and her posture. No. We were shocked because every ballet class in our collective memory had started at the barre. Not Petra's. She led us in a series of arm swings and shifts of weight from leg to leg—to establish range of motion and center of gravity, she explained. She circled the room, oozing enthusiasm, and asked each of us our name and our favorite ballet step. As the class progressed, she worked each person's choice into the exercises.

At the end of class, Petra said, "It was my pleasure to teach you this morning, girls. Thank you for sharing your energy so generously. I look forward to working with such a gifted group of movers over the coming weeks."

We gaped at each other as we filed into the change room. *It was my pleasure. Thank you for sharing.* No one had spoken to us like this before. We were all in so much shock that the tensions from yesterday were forgotten for the moment. We gathered on the lawn to eat lunch and pool our knowledge: Petra studied with Ms. Kelly up until five years ago. She belongs to the Vancouver company Ballet Now. She also creates and performs her own work as an independent choreographer. Ms. Kelly persuaded her to come and teach us on her summer break.

Sasha was half lying down, propped on an elbow. "She seems kind of fake to me." She pulled up a piece of grass and chewed it.

"Yeah," Jamie said. She was holding herself in plank position, balanced on forearms and toes, her elbows and ankles at right angles. Her biceps bulged.

"What do you mean?" I asked.

"I don't know," Sasha said. "Kind of airy-fairy."

"I think she's great," Lisa said. "She's really encouraging. We could use more of that around here."

"What do *you* think?" Sasha looked straight at me. It felt like she didn't want to soil her tongue with my name.

"It's too early to say for sure—"

Jamie sneered. "Cop out!"

"But so far, so good."

Sasha spat out the chewed piece of grass.

Lisa looked at her watch. "It's almost time." Our break lasted only forty-five minutes. "What's happening after lunch?"

I pulled out a crumpled paper schedule from my bag. "It just says, 'Rehearsal.'"

In the studio, Petra was trying out some movement and consulting a sheet of handwritten notes. Ms. Kelly carried her observation chair to the front of the room and said, "Petra has agreed to set a piece on you senior girls for the showing." She sat down and folded her hands. Her eyebrows arched in anticipation.

Petra seemed to emerge from a trance. She did a double-take when she saw Ms. Kelly in the observation chair. "I'm sorry, but I can't work like this."

Ms. Kelly's mouth dropped open. "What do you mean?"

"You're welcome to watch the piece when it's finished, but during the creative process, I hope you'll understand—I need to be alone with the dancers."

Ms. Kelly flushed. She glanced back and forth from us to

Petra as if debating what to say. Finally, she stood and lifted her chair. The cushion, tied only to the back rungs, hung straight down. Ms. Kelly looked so hurt and offended that I almost felt sorry for her. Still, when she marched out, her high heels clicking, it felt like the prison warden had gone off duty.

First, we lay on our backs and closed our eyes. Petra told us to release our weight into the floor, to feel the heaviness in our limbs. We took deep breaths and imagined sending the air into any tight spots, then we blew out the tension. She told us to isolate one part of our bodies and focus our attention on it. How did it feel—was it sore, relaxed, twitchy? Did it want to move? In what way?

"Let the impulse arise from within," Petra said. "Shut off your mind. Let the body part lead." I had picked my right foot, so I circled my ankle, pointed and flexed my toes, and shook it. I was glad we kept our eyes closed. No one could see how dorky my moves were.

Petra told us to imagine that we weren't in a dance studio, but lying in bed on Sunday morning. Would we roll over, would we extend a toe outside the covers to test the temperature in the room? What would our sleepy, relaxed bodies want to express? It felt gooey and luxurious. I stretched my arms above my head. I reached the soles of my feet to the ceiling and let my legs flop down one by one. I rolled and squirmed.

She instructed us to stand, keeping our eyes closed, and to remain still until a movement impulse surfaced within us. "You may find that your body feels programmed to move a certain way. That's normal. You're advanced dancers with years of training. Allow yourself to move in that habitual way—whether it's pointing and flexing, pliés, jazz isolations, whatever. Keep repeating the movement until you recognize that it's a pattern, it's something you learned. Then ask yourself, what's underneath it? What happens if you release your limbs from the grooves of habit? What do they have to say for themselves?"

Pretending to lie in bed freed me, but when I stood up, my limbs got stuck, just like she said. I couldn't seem to break out of my rut until Petra said, "Imagine you're swimming in a pool filled with Jell-O."

The air thickened and my limbs pressed against it. It felt like make-believe, not dancing. Petra kept giving us cues—"Now the Jell-O dissolves into mist; the wind is blowing so hard you can barely stand up"—and I responded from my gut. Minutes later, I opened my eyes as if waking up after a night of vivid dreams.

We sat cross-legged in a circle. Petra hugged her knees to her chest and clasped her wrist. "Improvisation will help you to develop a new dimension in your dancing. We'll also use these exercises to generate movement. You, as dancers, will help to build the piece. You're co-creators." Petra smiled and made eye contact with each of us in turn, her green eyes luminous.

When we were leaving the studio, Ms. Kelly stepped out of the office. She had probably spent the whole afternoon looking for a knothole in the wall to spy on us. She crossed her arms and inspected us as we traipsed past her to the change room. I caught her eye by accident. "Did you enjoy yourself, Natalie?"

I flattened my voice to sound casual. "It was all right."

But it was much more than all right. Inside, I was soaring.

Wednesday, July 14th

This morning, Ms. Kelly taught ballet again. The adagio was set to somber music and involved a lot of slow *ports de bras*. My arms seemed to push through water. As I stretched over my front leg in the lunge, I let my torso soften instead of holding it stiff like I usually do. This meant my fingertips actually swept the floor. I rose in one fluid motion, arms outstretched and framing my head, then arched backwards, my shoulders wide and my chest open. For once, Ms. Kelly didn't criticize me, but she gave me a weird look. Lisa leaned into me and whispered, "That was beautiful."

The compliment startled me, and I jerked my head towards Lisa. She nodded, as if trying to convince me. "Really."

"Thanks."

Later, in jazz class, Ms. Kelly hounded me. She had just started to lead the warm-up to a pounding rock beat when she spun around and pointed the remote at the stereo. Silence filled the room.

"Natalie. Go change."

I was wearing wide-legged sweat pants and a T-shirt. "All I have is my ballet gear—it's soaked."

She strode to her desk in the back corner of the studio and snatched up a flyer. "May I remind you of the studio rules?" She folded back the first page of the pamphlet and smoothed the crease between her thumb and index finger. "Rule number four: *Close-fitting clothes must be worn for all classes except Stretch and Conditioning.* When you registered at this studio, you agreed to abide by the rules. I'll overlook it this time, but I suggest you do laundry tonight."

In the past, when Ms. Kelly pissed me off, anger sharpened my lines, made me spin faster and jump higher. It ricocheted through my body and left me feeling roughed up and edgy, like I'd been in a fight.

It doesn't work anymore. Today, her attack made me sloppy. I couldn't control my limbs. You can imagine how well that went over with Sergeant Kelly. I think it reinforced her theory that loose-fitting clothes are the root of all evil.

Thursday, July 15th

I phoned Dad tonight. He sounded surprised because I usually call on the weekend. Well, tough. I'm not always going to stay in the little box he wants to keep me in.

"I miss you."

"I miss you too, honey," he said.

But when I suggested that he come out and visit, he said, "You know it works better when you girls come out here." He just means it's more convenient for him.

"So why can't I go out there next month?"

"We already discussed this." He sounded tired. "You came out by yourself last year, and now it's Paige's turn."

"But what am I going to do? I'll be lonely out here."

"You'll have your mom all to yourself."

"Ha! You know what that's like. She has her nose in a book 24/7."

"What about your friends? How's that friend of yours ... Hannah?"

"Sasha, Dad, her name's Sasha. Is it that hard to remember? I don't go around calling your girlfriend Vicky or Veronica."

He chuckled at that. "You know I'm bad with names."

"It doesn't matter. *Sasha* isn't speaking to me."

The conversation dragged on, and I wasn't feeling any happier by the time I hung up. Mom keeps asking if I'm going to the cabin with her and Marine next month. She says maybe I could stay with Grandma in Courtenay for part of the week if the cabin idea turns me off. But Paige and I visited Grandma on spring break. I haven't seen Dad in a *year!*

Friday, July 16th

As Ms. Kelly watched us stream out of the studio after Petra's rehearsal today, she said, "Where are your pointe shoes?"

Jamie, who happens to be incredibly good at pointe (her feet are just as strong as the rest of her), told her we weren't using them. "We're learning a modern piece."

Ms. Kelly pursed her lips and marched into the studio. We overheard her confront Petra. Turns out she assumed that Petra would set a pointe piece on us. She hadn't intended for Petra to introduce us to modern at all. Before long, Ms. Kelly barged into the change room and ordered all of us to leave, except Jamie.

While we waited in the parking lot, Lisa reviewed the choreography. Sasha crammed her fists into the pockets of her hoodie and kicked at the gravel. We've barely talked since Kevin's accident. I was figuring out what to say to her when Jamie burst out the door and ran up to us. "I'm doing a pointe solo in the showing!"

"Right on!" Lisa high-fived Jamie.

"Congratulations," I said.

Sasha shoved Jamie. "You're such a bunhead!"

Rehearsals for our group piece continue in bare feet.

Saturday, July 17th

This evening I biked to The Ice Cream Place. Claire was working, and I hadn't visited her since she started the job. The place was swarming with customers. When Claire saw me, she glanced at the long line ahead of me and shrugged an apology. I watched her scoop for awhile—she has already built up her muscles and she gauges cone sizes expertly—then claimed a table on the sidewalk.

Cars rumbled in and out of the parking lot and exhaust fumes had nearly driven me back inside when a Camaro rolled up. It was full of guys I'd crossed paths with at Sasha's—friends of Kevin's. They cruised the parking lot and pulled into a spot. Two of them jumped out and headed for the store. I ducked my head. There wasn't much chance that they would recognize me, but still. "Look at that line-up!" one of them said. "Screw this. Let's just head."

"What time was Kev supposed to meet us?"

"At eight—it's twenty after now."

They paused beside my table. "Have you seen a guy hanging around here, about yea high, curly hair, looks kind of like Rafael Nadal?"

"Curly hair? Looks like Nadal? What, are you in love with him, faggot?"

The guy who had described Kevin shoved the other one. "Who're you calling faggot? Takes one to know one, faggot!"

They wrestled until I thought they'd forgotten about me. But when the first one finally broke free, he turned to me. "Guess you haven't seen anyone who fits that description?"

"Sorry. Maybe you should try the tennis courts."

"She's a riot, eh, Brad? Hey, what are you doing out here by yourself? Want to come party with us?"

The guy named Brad took his friend by the elbow. "You've got to excuse Tyler. He can't decide whether he's a fag or a pedophile tonight."

"What do you mean pedophile? She's old enough!"

At that moment, the driver yelled out the window of the Camaro and the guys took off just as Claire appeared with a hot fudge sundae. "Were they bothering you?" She watched the car peel away. Despite the apron and puffy, short-sleeved blouse, she looked ready to defend me.

"I think I held my own."

Claire led me around back to a staff picnic area bordered by a couple of pine bushes. She offered me a spoon to share the sundae, but I thought about those spandex unitards and shook my head.

"Are you sure?" She shrugged and helped herself. It didn't look as though working in an ice cream store had hurt her figure any.

"We miss you at the studio."

"I hate to say it, but I don't miss the studio that much. I miss the girls, but—I'm having fun this summer. I feel so much older now that I have a job. And I met this guy …"

"Really?"

"He kept coming into the store. I was like, no one eats that much ice cream! When I bugged him about it, he got really red—it's so cute when he blushes—and asked me out. We ride our bikes everywhere and play tennis and stuff. His older sister has a car and sometimes we go places with her and her boyfriend. We're all going camping next weekend."

Claire's coworker called for help and she left the sundae behind. A breeze stirred the bushes and the smell of pine sap took me back to the lake. The rough planks of the picnic table turned into the wooden dock. The memory of lying there with Kevin stirred me up inside. I felt a tingling in my crotch and wanted … him. What did it mean? Was I a slut like Sasha said? What Claire had described with her boyfriend sounded so innocent and safe. Not like what I had done with Kevin. Slut, tramp, whore, slut, tramp, whoreslutrampwhoreslutrampwhore …

I found myself staring at the bottom of an empty ice cream dish. I had grabbed the half-eaten sundae and wolfed it down until chocolate burned the back of my throat. Nausea pulled me out of my trance. What a relief it would be to throw up. There was a name for that: bulimia. We saw a film about it in Health class. Well, I'm not interested in turning bulimic. I just need to start exercising some self-restraint.

I threw away the dish and strolled back to my bike. As I was unlocking it, someone said my name.

I turned and stared: Kevin in the flesh. For a split second, I thought I was imagining him. I shivered to shake off the dream. He leaned back on his bike, one hand resting on the seat, the other on the handlebars. The position pushed his shoulders into a shrug.

"Hey. How you doing?" he said.

"I'm okay. How are you?"

"I've been better." He wrinkled his forehead. "Maybe you heard?"

"Yeah." Talking to Kevin made me feel exposed and prickly. It was hard to hold up my end of the conversation, and all I really wanted to do was ride away. "Do you have a court date yet?"

"Still waiting."

I searched for something to say and remembered the Camaro. "Some of your friends came by here looking for you."

He glanced at his watch. "I missed them, huh?"

"You don't sound too disappointed."

"Ever since the accident, those guys' idea of fun seems more and more like a death wish. You know?"

"I can imagine."

He shuddered as if to put it all behind him. "What are *you* doing out by yourself on a Saturday night?"

"That's a popular question."

He smirked. His eyes reminded me so much of Sasha's that I blurted, "My best friend suddenly stopped talking to me."

"You mean my sister?"

I nodded. Kevin bent his head as if to scan the ground. "Things are pretty crazy at home right now. You shouldn't take it personally." He hesitated, then raised his head. "Look, Natalie, you've known our family for a long time, but—"

Claire bounced back outside. "Sorry! Usually I get at least fifteen minutes." She noticed Kevin and added, "Oh! Hi."

"Nat and I are just heading off on a sunset bike tour. Want to join us?"

I glared at him: *the nerve.* Claire would think Kevin and I had planned to meet here—that we were on a date. But if she felt surprised, it didn't show. "I'd love to, but I have to work for another hour." She winked at me as she gathered abandoned ice cream dishes. "Have fun!"

"Don't look at me like that!" Kevin said as soon as Claire was out of earshot. "As long as we're both on bikes, we might as well ride together. Besides, I know a great route." He put his helmet on. "You coming?"

I shrugged and donned my helmet. He led the way down alleys I didn't know existed, along dirt paths so narrow that salal branches scratched my arms and legs, and up steep hills that led to glorious stretches of downhill coasting. Wind whipped past. Gardens scented the evening air: cedar, jasmine, honeysuckle. At times I didn't even know where we were. When he called over his shoulder, "Having fun, Natalie?" I squealed in reply.

We must have been riding for close to an hour. We were scaling a big hill and I was just getting ready to demand a break—the guy is in *great* shape!—when the path spat us out onto rocks, bald except for moss and broom bushes. He screeched to a halt and I veered just in time to avoid a crash. He grabbed the frame of my bike. The rocks fell away to streets, houses, and ocean far below. The air had thickened, somehow. Dusk hung in it like fog.

"Turn around."

The sky blazed fuchsia. The disc of sun slipped, second by second, behind purple hills on the horizon. Clouds sponged the light and the sky shimmered peach, pink, yellow, and even green. A plume of airplane exhaust twisted vertically, like a tornado. With every breath, the colors changed. The brilliance faded, slowly, and left us standing in the dark.

The last time I'd been alone with Kevin at night, we were parked in his car. He'd pulled me towards him and kissed me. Would he make a move now? My bike stood between us, like a wall. I casually rolled my wheels back to open up a passage way.

He snapped his head at the motion. "Ready to go?"

So much for romance.

Then it hit me. "I've got no light!" We were miles from home.

"Don't worry. I know this neighborhood even better in the dark."

The ground was rapidly disappearing underfoot. "What do you mean?"

"I was a bike-riding outlaw for years before I ever had a driver's license. This takes me back to my roots."

I stayed close to his rear wheel as we wound down narrow, unlit streets. When we hit the major roads with their streetlights, he sped up. I played it safe and hung back. I didn't want to hit a pothole, or a cat—or get hit by a car, for that matter. But then the distance widened between us.

What the hell? I pedaled harder. I caught up to Kevin's rear reflector so that we were almost riding tandem. Keeping pace with his skinny-tired road bike on my mountain bike nearly killed me. I was so absorbed that I paid no attention to where we were going. My street loomed up and surprised me. Before I could call out, Kevin swerved. He *did* know his way around. He escorted me to my driveway, where we stopped, and he balanced, his feet wedged in toe clips. Finally, he wobbled too far off center. He freed one foot just in time to catch his fall and ended up close enough to hear my huffing and puffing.

He laughed. "Need to add a little cardio to the routine, hey?" He leaned forward—moving in for a kiss? I gasped. He pressed two fingers against my throat and held them still as I gulped air. "Your pulse is dangerously fast! I'm serious."

At least it was too dark for him to see me blush.

He let his hand fall. "Maybe we should do that again some time. Get you in shape. I could be your personal trainer."

I was gaining control of my breath. "Get real! Have you *seen* what I'm riding? Look at how fat these tires are. Let's just switch bikes next time. I'll kick your ass."

He dropped his chin to his neck and grinned at the ground. "That sounds like fun." He mounted his bike. "So long, Natalie."

He rounded the corner and vanished. I didn't know where

he was staying or when I might see him again. I stood in the driveway long enough for my heart to slow down, then stowed my bike and headed for the shower.

Sunday, July 18th

This morning I woke up to the sound of a softball landing in a glove, mixed with Paige's chatter. The soft noises drifted through my bedroom window, much more pleasant than the squawk of an alarm clock. Sunday: nowhere to go. I stretched and resettled, then remembered: this kind of movement was Petra's raw material. As I rolled and flopped, I paid attention in a new way.

A deeper voice rumbled in response to Paige's. I flung off the covers and pried the blinds apart. Paige was playing catch on the front lawn with a man I'd never seen before. I pulled on shorts and ran outside. "Paige!"

"Hi, Nat. You're finally up. Mom says teenagers need more sleep than anybody else, but I don't see why."

The man chuckled and looked at Paige like she was the most adorable thing he'd ever seen.

"Who are you?"

He shifted the ball to his left hand and stuck out his arm. I ignored it until he let it fall to his side. "Phil Ainslie. My parents live across the street; you must have met them?"

I looked at this Phil person more closely: salt and pepper hair, receding hairline, a paunch forming over the waistband of his Bermuda shorts. "There's an old couple across the street," I said.

"That's right, they're my parents. They moved out here to retire. I'm just visiting. from Ontario. Got here last night. They're having a rest right now, and I was just heading out for a walk when your sister here," he winked at Paige, "asked me to play catch with her."

I put my hand on Paige's shoulder. "Ontario. Isn't that a little far? What happens when there's an emergency? You're not much good to them way out there. We had snow this winter, you know. I saw your dad out there shoveling and I was a little worried about him. He could have keeled over from a heart attack." I was getting off topic. "Do you always play with little girls?"

Phil's expression hardened. He set the ball down on the grass and backed away. "I'm sorry I intruded. I wouldn't have done this back home, but it seems so small town here, I thought a person could be neighborly without—"

Paige whined. "He was playing with me!"

"*I'll* play with you." I picked up the ball and let it smack against my palm several times, as if it might come in handy as a weapon to bean Phil's head. He kept retreating until he reached the pavement, then he turned and strode back to his parents' house. Apparently, he'd changed his mind about the walk.

Paige placed her fists on her hips. "Why were you so mean to him?"

"I'll get Mom to explain it. Come around to the back."

"Hey! You said you'd play with me."

"I will, I will, just let me eat breakfast first. Mom!" I sprinted to the back porch with Paige in tow. Mom was stretched out on the chaise longue, a hardcover book propped open on her stomach, a glass of orange juice in one hand. "Mom! While you're back here reading yourself senseless, your ten-year-old daughter is out front playing with a creepy old man!"

Paige protested. "He wasn't creepy!"

I left Paige and Mom to sort things out and shut the sliding glass door behind me. I grabbed a box of bran flakes and shook it into a bowl. A strainer filled with rinsed raspberries sat next to the sink. I dropped a few berries onto my cereal and stirred in some milk. Boring. When Dad lived with us, he made pancakes on Sunday. I stared past my bowl at the phone.

Dear Dad,
All you are to me is a voice, tinny and two dimensional. We can't do stuff together. I never see you. I don't even think of you as flesh and blood anymore.

And it's all your fault. You chose to move 3,000 miles away. Nobody made you.

Damn it. Don't you miss me?

Don't answer that. You don't deserve to see me. You don't deserve a daughter, let alone two.

I couldn't finish my cereal. My stomach cramped up. I stormed back out to the porch, where Mom was just settling back into her book.

"I hope this makes you realize how dangerous it is when a little girl grows up without a father. She's a sitting duck for any man who pays attention to her."

Mom held her place in her book with an index finger and pushed her sunglasses into her hair. We looked each other in the eye. "Don't you think you're overreacting? We know who the Ainslies are."

"That's not the point. He could have been anyone! And you,

did you even know he was out there? Why don't you wake up and do your job as a mom?"

At that, Mom carefully placed her bookmark between the pages, shut her novel, and stood up. I didn't know what she was doing.

She bent over the wooden side of the balcony. She was wearing shorts, for a change, made of sage green cotton. When she rose on tiptoe, her calf muscles rippled. Apart from a few varicose veins, her legs are still in decent shape. It annoys me that they're thinner than mine. "Paige?"

Paige responded from down below. "What?"

"Do you want to play catch?"

"With who?"

Mom winced, as if Paige's response confirmed her guilt. "With me."

Paige didn't say anything for a second. "You mean you want me to teach you? Okay!" She ran to the foot of the stairs. "I can show you everything I've learned at softball camp!" Holding the banister, Mom glanced back at me and raised her eyebrows.

She was admitting I was right. I'd won.

So why did I feel so bad?

Monday, July 19th

Ms. Kelly kicked me out of the studio today. Every jazz class, she has harassed me, and today she finally said, "Natalie, we only have four rehearsals left before the showing. I've been waiting for you to get over your slump, but it's just not happening. You're putting the other dancers in jeopardy. I'll have to take you out of the piece if you can't turn your attitude around—and I mean *all* the way around."

I couldn't believe she was interrupting rehearsal to chew me out in front of the other girls. I had actually semi-enjoyed the warm-up, and we had only run the dance once. "What did I do?"

"It's what you're not doing, Natalie. You're half the dancer you used to be. You're one of the most advanced dancers in the school and people used to look up to you. But now you act bored and ..." She paused, her hands on her hips. She was wearing gold spandex pants, a white blouse open over a leotard and knotted at the waist, and white jazz shoes. A pair of high-heeled sandals lay on the floor beside the stereo—she would slip into those after class, as if she had Barbie-doll feet. She always wears full makeup—foundation, blush, the works, like she's about to go on stage. She must be close to Mom's age. "And you seem disgusted! As though the movement is beneath you."

I muttered, "Just because I don't want to look like a slut ..." I don't think Ms. Kelly heard me, but some girls nearby tittered. She definitely heard them.

"Your attitude is damaging the morale of the class and setting a bad example for the younger girls. You're excused for the rest of the day. I suggest you go home and think about your behavior."

"Fine," I snapped. As I passed Lisa, she mouthed, "I'll call you."

I changed into my shorts and hurried down the street. In the window of Con Brio, Petra was bent over a notebook, twisting a strand of blonde hair around her finger. Every so often she jotted something down with a pencil. I entered the café and approached her. She raised her head and smiled. Her sea green T-shirt set off her tan and her platinum hair so well, it took my breath away. She glanced at her watch. "It's not like Ms. Kelly to end class early."

"She kicked me out of the studio."

Petra hooked the barstool beside her with her foot and pulled it out. "Have a seat. What happened?"

As I explained, Petra frowned and fidgeted with her gold necklace. "I think this might have something to do with me. I've been raving to Ms. Kelly about your facility with modern."

"You have?" I felt too shy to look at her. I knew I felt a deep connection with Petra's movement style, but I had no idea whether or not it showed. As far as I could tell, she praised everyone equally.

"Oh, yes, Natalie. You're a natural. I try not to play favorites in class, but under the circumstances, it's only fair to tell you. You're very talented."

Ms. Kelly's insults and Petra's compliments tumbled in my head. Criticism was familiar, but I didn't know how to handle flattery. It seemed safest to let it slide off me without taking it to heart.

"You probably know she wasn't too happy about my setting a modern piece in the first place. Maybe she feels that you've transferred your loyalty."

I heard Ms. Kelly's words in my head: *You act as though the movement is beneath you.* "I just don't like her style of jazz anymore. It makes me feel sort of like a machine, or an object. A sex object, I guess."

I wasn't sure Petra would know what I meant, but she nodded. A couple of men in shorts and baseball caps entered the café and rubber-necked at Petra. She didn't seem to notice them. "That style of jazz started in the showgirl industry in Las Vegas and L.A. It's all about pleasing customers. Artistic expression hardly enters into it. Frankly, I'm surprised she hasn't phased it out by now."

I slouched on the stool, chin propped in my hand. I was thinking what a relief it would be to quit dance: I could scoop ice cream and ride my bike. This was the last week of the intensive. Maybe I should just drop out.

Petra touched my arm. "I'm thrilled with your work in my piece, Natalie. I really hope that you'll keep coming to my ballet class and to rehearsal for the rest of the week."

An iced latte might perk me up. The men who had ogled Petra were waiting for their drinks. Mustached and leathery-skinned, they tried to catch my eye. I ordered, then pretended to be lost in thought.

"You from around here?" one of them said.

I couldn't ignore a direct question. I nodded.

"We're just visiting from the States."

You don't say.

"You a ballet dancer?" the other one said.

That made my head turn. "How did you know?" For a second I thought maybe they recognized Petra.

The ham-fisted tourist reached over and patted the bun of hair at the back of my head. I ducked and twisted away from him, protecting my head and neck with both hands.

"How about introducing us to your friend?" the other one said.

Adrenaline flooded my veins and my face felt hot. I was on the verge of telling them to fuck off when the barista rolled her eyes in sympathy and passed me my drink. She had made mine first. "Thank you so much."

"Anytime."

I plunked too much money on the counter and didn't wait for change.

It took me a few cool sips to recover. That jerk had some nerve patting my head. Petra agreed. The men passed us on their way outside to the smoking area. We pretended they didn't exist.

When I got home, Lisa called. She urged me to stay in the show. "It may be our last chance to perform together!" she said. "Besides, you love Petra's piece."

Mom overheard me talking to Lisa and got pretty worked up. "Who does that woman think she is? She has no right to expel you from a single *class*, let alone threaten to cut you out of a piece in the show. I should get your father to call her up and remind her of how much money he's poured into her school over the years. Of all the nerve!"

Mom gets fired up about injustice. It makes her want to fight back. But my fighting spirit is broken, at least where Ms. Kelly is concerned. So tomorrow I'm sleeping in.

Tuesday, July 20th

This morning the phone rang as I was shuffling into the kitchen, barely awake. Mom was taking a shower. I thought about letting the machine pick up, but habit won. I answered.

"Natalie, is that you? It's Ms. Kelly from Dance-Is."

My system jolted into high alert. "This is Natalie."

"I'm sorry for losing my patience yesterday. Of course I want you in the jazz piece. I just want to see a bit of the old Nat—the old fire. Deal?"

I held my breath and looked at the calendar above the phone. Four days to go.

"Okay?" I detected desperation in her voice.

"I talked to Petra," I said.

"Yes? And?"

"And I'm going to keep working with her."

"That's great." She paused. "But we need you in the jazz piece too. Forget what I said yesterday."

My stomach swirled and my knees trembled. I planted my hand on the kitchen counter as a word sliced across my mind. "No. I'll do Petra's class and her rehearsal, but that's it."

When I hung up, my head swam. It reminded me of the caffeine rush after a latte.

"Who was that?" Mom walked into the kitchen in her bathrobe.

"You can't fire me, I quit!"

Mom toweled her hair, looking puzzled.

Wednesday, July 21st

I'm lying on my bed in shorts and a tank top with the window open. The air smells the way a glass of water tastes when you're really thirsty. A slight breeze tickles my bare arms and legs. My quilt is bunched up to one side. I'm waiting to see how much cooler it has to get before it's more comfortable to pull the covers over me than to lie here without them. The cordless phone rests in my palm and I keep twirling it. I can't decide whether or not to call Sasha.

Things between us aren't as bad as they were that day in the change room when she refused to speak in my presence, let alone *to* me. We say hi to each other. She doesn't seem very happy, though. The family obviously wasn't getting along that well before Kevin's accident, and now tensions must run that much higher. Aside from the drunk driving, Kevin wasn't even supposed to be living there this summer. He had planned to be up north making money so he could move out in the fall. I remember Sasha telling me how much she was looking forward to that. It's pretty tight quarters in their town house, and I think she and Kevin fight a lot.

He was so mellow when we rode our bikes together. He wasn't even smoking or chewing anything. When we watched the sunset, I wanted him to hold me. Other memories—the lake memories—make my heart race, whether from excitement or fear, I can't tell. Maybe both. Maybe I *am* "old enough." I've had my period for a whole year. That means I'm biologically a woman, right?

God, what am I saying? See, this is why I can't phone Sasha's house. I don't know what I might get myself into if Kevin answers. It's much too scary. If we're going to make up, it will have to be at the studio.

Thursday, July 22nd

Tonight we went to the closing softball game at Paige's summer camp. Mom's friend Marine came along. When Paige invited her to watch a game that day at the library, I didn't expect her to take it seriously. She must be pretty hard up for entertainment. On the other hand, she obviously loves the sport. Every time anyone on Paige's team hit the ball, caught it, or advanced to the next base, Marine led the cheers. Paige looked great in her blue and white costume—I mean, uniform. When her team won, we jumped to our feet, waved our arms, and yelled.

In a diner after the game, Paige and I claimed one side of the booth, Mom and Marine the other. Kids versus grown-ups, the way we used to sit when Dad and Mom were married. Now, though, I don't seem to fit on either side of the table.

Paige ordered a veggie-burger platter. While I was picking at my green salad, I stared at her fries. Their edges were jagged as though cut with pinking shears, and I wanted to feel the hot, greasy ridges on my tongue, to taste the pulpy potato inside. Puberty hasn't struck Paige yet. Her skin remains pimple-free, her body unbloated.

For dessert, she ordered a banana split. It came with four spoons so that we could all share it. Maybe I shouldn't have cared, since I'm not performing in the jazz number this weekend, but I kept visualizing myself in that scarlet unitard. I imagined the ice cream particles traveling directly to my chunky calves and saddlebag thighs and taking up permanent residence. Mom didn't help. She said, "Dig in!" like a crazed archaeologist and thrust a spoon at me.

To distract myself, I asked Marine about her name. She lit up as if that was her favorite question.

"My parents named me Maureen, but I changed it because I like the sea and the color blue." Check: she was wearing a turquoise blouse with a white collar, a white breast pocket, and large white buttons. Her blunt haircut and wing-shaped glasses echoed the angular patterns on her clothes. I had to admit, the lady had style.

"Your blouse is funky," I said.

Marine beamed. Mom looked over, a spoonful of ice cream hovering in front of her mouth, then glanced away, as if she didn't want to jinx the moment. I realized that I could avoid eating my portion of the sundae by taking an interest in Marine.

"Did you make it yourself?"

It turns out that Marine makes and sells clothes, and she's also a painter. She teaches art at an alternative school, where they don't give grades. She encourages her students to express themselves and doesn't evaluate or judge. Now that I'm working with Petra, Marine's ideas don't sound so dumb.

Marine swallowed a spoonful of ice cream. "This banana split is *bliss*."

I thumped my water glass on the table and glared at Mom. "Sorry, Nat."

Marine darted her eyes back and forth from me to Mom. "Did I say something wrong?"

"It's okay," Mom said. "It's just—we avoid that word."

Marine set down her spoon and looked at the sundae. "Banana split?"

"No."

"Oh, bl—the other *b* word?"

"That's the one. I'll explain later."

I glared at Mom again. I didn't want her talking about me behind my back. Dad's selfish pursuit of "bliss" didn't deserve any more air time, either.

"No need to explain," Marine said. "From now on, I banish that word from my vocabulary. Poof! Gone. Didn't need it anyway." Her tone was so reassuring that I relaxed and lounged against the booth.

Friday, July 23rd

Almost time for dress rehearsal. Ms. Kelly's going to find out that I'm not half, but *twice* the dancer I used to be. Of course, Petra's piece will probably look messy and unfinished to her. There's not much unison, we work in turned-in positions, the lines of our arms and legs are often soft, not sharp—we actually *try* to look like spaghetti at one point, an image Ms. Kelly only ever uses as an insult. Also, we're performing in wide-legged pants. She'll sniff and ask us if we're supposed to be at a pajama party. But I don't care. I bet Mom will like it.

Saturday, July 24th

The good, the bad, the ugly.

Backstage (that is, in the high school locker room) before the show, all the other senior girls were pulling on their red unitards for the jazz piece. The modern piece was in the second half, so I kept my sweats on. I was taking time with my makeup and trying hard not to feel left out. I had never missed out on a piece before. Lisa was keeping me company, though she had pulled a hamstring and was a little preoccupied. I offered her some tiger balm, and the smells of menthol and camphor spread as she rubbed it into her leg.

A few lockers away, Sasha was talking quietly to Jamie, with her back to me. Jamie kept darting glances at me.

"Pee-ew, smells like moth balls in here," Sasha said over her shoulder.

I concentrated on applying eyeliner. In the mirror, I saw Sasha turn around.

"I think Ms. Kelly realizes that some people just shouldn't wear unitards. They're not flattering to everyone," she said. "It's so easy to put on five or ten pounds, but unitards don't let you get away with anything. You're so lucky you don't have to wear one of these, Natalie."

I gave her a fake smile. How come I never noticed how catty she is? I used to play along, of course. I hate to think of how many times we would phone each other up and say, "Did you see what so-and-so was wearing today? Doesn't she know that people with olive skin can't wear pink? And how about that lipstick? Talk about fire-engine red. It totally clashed with her sweater!"

I was still searching for a comeback when Lisa spoke up. "Having us all wear identical unitards is supposed to create a group identity. From a design perspective, it's supposed to unite us, not divide us."

That was much better than I could have done. Lisa rocks.

"How does your leg feel, Lisa?"

"Warm and tingly. Thanks for the balm." She wiggled her hips and swung her leg back and forth in its socket.

Jamie grabbed Sasha and the two of them pranced by. Sasha hooked Lisa's elbow. "Come on, Lisa, we're on soon."

Lisa squeezed my hand and looked me in the eyes.

"*Merde*," I said.

"*Merde*."

I found a spot in the wings so that I wouldn't be around when the jazz piece ended and the girls came streaming back into the change room, giggling and complaining: "You stepped on my foot!" "Could you believe that guy hooting in the balcony?" "What the hell happened to the CD? Did it skip, or what?"

I stayed there throughout the junior girls' jazz number, Jamie's solo, and the junior girls' ballet number, stretching and bouncing to keep warm. When the time came for the modern piece, I joined the other girls on stage. As the music started and the curtain rose, I disappeared into the piece. For eight and a half minutes, I melded with the movement, the other dancers, the wooden boards under my feet.

We lay intertwined as the lights came up. Slowly, we began to rustle and shift. Crouched in a ball, one girl raised her back into a cat arch and let it fall. Another lifted an arm and let it drift back down. On my stomach, I snaked in a wave, then pushed into a downward dog pose—hands and feet pressed into the floor, head down, hips high. Gradually, the others rose and began a repetitive motion—Jamie held both arms together as if wielding an ax and swung them down, her arms parting at the bottom of the stroke and smoothing the air to touch Sasha's head. Half squatting, half kneeling, Sasha rolled back on herself to stand up. Her left arm reached overhead and drove down as if dunking a basket. Lisa made a circle of her arms, caught the impulse, and spun. I joined in. Backed by a soundtrack of major chords, we formed a kind of assembly line.

The lights brightened, and our movement expanded. One by one, we took solos along an arcing pathway in front of the group. While each girl claimed center stage, the rest of us bore each other's weight, then let ourselves be supported. Everyone worked together. To finish, the soloist rejoined the line at the opposite end. Her arrival cued the next dancer to peel off. We adjusted our spacing to fill in the gap that each left.

During Sasha's solo, the music changed. It pulsed and sped up, became more frenetic. In response, she jerked her arms and head and jumped erratically. Soon her solo time had elapsed, but she didn't return to the line. The music turned into noise— shattering glass, thunderclaps, distorted voice-overs like military orders. The group splintered. In spokes, we tumbled, rolled, leapt, and dove. We narrowly missed colliding until one by one our pathways led us into the wings.

In twos, threes, or alone, we crisscrossed the stage. In pairs, girls pushed, shoved, and tripped each other. In a trio, two ganged up on the third, either trapping her or shutting her out. When I crossed the stage alone, I staggered, disoriented, searching the ceiling. Loneliness welled to the surface and sapped my strength. My legs weighed me down. I was rooted to the spot, barely able to move. *This wasn't choreographed. I was wrecking the dance.* I lagged behind the music until, with a panicked surge of effort, I propelled myself to the other side.

A change in music renewed my energy. All of us entered and circled each other. We picked up speed and started to race. What would happen if someone couldn't run with the pack?

Lisa tripped and fell. The survivors scattered and kept circling. A sparring match broke out between Sasha and Jamie. The rest of us clapped like an audience at a cock fight until Jamie knocked Sasha down.

I knelt over Sasha, held her head, and helped her pull herself into a crouch. With my arm to support her, she rose to her feet, and Jamie backed away. Sasha and I returned to Lisa, who revived at our approach and climbed into a chair we made by joining our hands at the wrists. She rode on our stretcher/throne. All of us returned to center stage to rebuild the opening tableau. We changed positions and reversed the gestures. Lisa slid to standing and assumed center stage. She planed the air, grazing my head in a caress, and then swept her arms overhead into a cone shape. Her palms touched each other in prayer.

My heart was pounding by the time the curtain fell. The crowd was hushed. They seemed in shock and had to rouse themselves to applaud. This wasn't the packaged entertainment they were used to. It was art. We held hands to take a bow. For a few seconds, Sasha and I stood hand-in-hand. But even before the curtain fell, she shook herself free.

Petra rushed backstage afterwards. I couldn't look at her. She was going to be so disappointed in me for screwing up the timing on my solo crossing. I hung back as she moved through the ranks, giving hugs and shaking hands. "Well done, Lisa! Way to go, Sasha!" I kept turning so that I faced away from her, but finally she ducked in front of me. "Nat, what's wrong?"

I covered my face with my hands. "I'm sorry about the crossing. I don't know what happened."

She rested her hand on my shoulder. "You were phenomenal, that's what happened!"

I peered at her through my fingers. "Seriously?"

"Nat, the entire audience was holding its breath at that moment. You made us *feel* the struggle. Do you know how hard that is? Most professional dancers never get there. It's one thing to be pleasing to look at; it's another thing to move the audience. You moved us."

I threw my arms around her. It's not that I believed her. But it was obvious that she wasn't mad at me. I was so relieved that I wanted to cry.

Petra corralled everyone into the lobby for group photos. After a few formal shots, we struck poses. I was making a blowfish expression—cheeks puffed out, eyes bugged—when I met Sasha's eyes and my face went slack. Her look was so bitter, it chilled me.

A friendly looking, gray-haired man stood next to Petra. She introduced him to me as Lance Irving. He wasn't very tall, but when he turned his attention on me, he seemed much larger. His deep blue eyes made me feel understood. He gripped my hand. "Lovely work."

I blushed. "Thank you."

"Natalie, Lance is moving to Victoria. He plans to teach modern here this fall," Petra said.

"If there's enough interest, that is," Lance said.

"You would love his class," Petra said. "I can't recommend it highly enough. I wouldn't be who I am today without Lance."

Lance hid his face. "Oh, stop." But when he moved his hands, his eyes were shining. I could see that, deep down, he accepted her praise.

"You can count on me, I know that," I said. "And I'll spread the word."

He tilted his head and nodded. "That's very kind."

Behind Lance, Ms. Kelly was greeting parents. Just then, she turned and saw me. She hesitated, then squared her shoulders and lunged in Lance's direction, her hand outstretched. I gave her a wan smile and turned away.

Mom and Paige approached and gave me a homemade bouquet of bluebells and daisies. I hugged them both. "I'll get changed and then we can get out of here," I said.

Alone on the senior side of the change room, Sasha was undoing her hair, her arms raised and her elbows pointed towards the walls, like she was about to do a sit-up. "Secret admirer?" Sasha said when she saw the flowers. "Kevin will be jealous."

"Give me a break, Sasha. They're from my mom and Paige."

"Must be nice."

It struck me that Sasha's parents hadn't been in the lobby. I'd taken it for granted that Kevin wouldn't come; he never attended any of her performances. But her mom always came, and her dad often joined her. What had happened tonight? I softened my voice. "Actually, it *is* nice."

Sasha turned away and rifled in her locker. I stepped out of my flowy pants and pulled on my jeans. Sasha's shoulder blades winged out as she bent forward, and the fine hairs on her neck caught the light. Her ribs rose and fell. Her legs pushed the ground away, lean and strong. But without Jamie at her side, she seemed smaller, almost fragile. She stopped moving. *I miss you*, I wanted to say. I was about to ask her if anything was wrong when she snapped, "Quit staring at me!"

"Sorry." She moved aside to reveal a mirror in the locker door, small and cracked but obviously still functional.

"Good show, Sasha. See you later."

"Sure. Have a nice life."

I took a step towards her. "Why are you so mad at me? Is this still about Kevin?"

Sasha was flinging her clothes off and on. It made me think of tears in motion. If she moved fast enough, she wouldn't have to cry. I knew she didn't want me to interrupt. "Call me if you want to talk, okay? Sasha?"

She slammed the locker shut and hoisted her pack to her back. She was going to beat me out the door. "Whatever."

I caught up with Mom and Paige and we escaped into the summer evening. Mom offered to take us out for dessert, but I opted for a walk on Willows Beach. We drove the short distance and cooled our feet on the sand—fine and silky, if you avoided driftwood and cigarette butts. The surf pulsed, the moon lit the water, and the air eddied around us. Paige grabbed a stick and ran ahead while Mom and I sauntered. When we caught up to her, she had written NAT RULES on the shore. I went to hug her and she shrieked, "No! You'll squeeze the stuffing out of me!" She ran around in circles and I chased her till Mom called, "Girls, girls! Calm down. It's dark down here and someone is going to get hurt." We collapsed on our backs and laughed up at the stars.

Wednesday, July 28th

Paige leaves tomorrow. As she packs, she keeps asking, "Do Dad and Violet have *Harry Potter*? What Wii games do they have?

Do they have flippers in my size at the cabin?" It's getting on my nerves. I told her not to assume they had anything to keep a ten-year-old girl entertained. Dad shed most signs of us when he moved to his new place. A couple of outdated pictures of Paige and me hang as evidence of his former life, but otherwise he was born again as a freewheeling divorcé. (How come that doesn't sound right? What's the word for a divorced man? There isn't one, is there? Mom would have a field day. It bugs me when she's right about stuff like that.)

It's just as well. I'm not sure I could stand to walk into his condo and see the clay bowl that I made in Grade One and proudly presented to him for Father's Day, my thumbprints still visible where I pinched the sides into shape, a matte patch where I missed with the glazing brush. I wonder what ever became of it? Dad's décor is what you would call minimalist. Bare walls; a big, black television; a couple of tall lamps that stand in the corners like awkward newcomers at a party. The only bit of character in the living room is contained in the black CD stands that climb the walls. Not the stands themselves, but the music inside them: jazz, blues, classical, and even some experimental electronic music and indie pop. Last summer, I worked my way through his CD collection as I danced in the living room. By myself.

Next week, Mom vacations at the cabin with Marine. I haven't talked to Sasha since the night of the show. Claire says The Ice Cream Place isn't hiring. Opportunities have dried up all over. The Summertime Blues strike again.

Thursday, July 29th

Paige chattered all the way to the airport, reporting what she'd read online in a kids' encyclopedia about air travel: security checkpoints, cabin pressure, landing strips, baggage handlers. She wore a pink Hello Kitty backpack and carried a stuffed unicorn under her arm. When I hugged her goodbye, my eyes teared up and hers widened. Great, I was upsetting her. Luckily, the flight attendant arrived just then with a hundred-watt smile on her face. Her white teeth actually sparkled like in the cartoons. They're probably veneers like Sasha and I saw on *Oprah*: People have their teeth whittled away to stumps and covered with ultra-white falsies. Fake teeth or not, the flight attendant obviously knew how to interact with kids. Paige perked right up again and hurried through the gate. The lady had to prompt her to turn and wave.

When we got home from the airport, Mom and I made egg sandwiches and green tea. As we ate, I was reading the paper, and she, totally out of character, wasn't reading anything. "Have you thought any more about inviting Sasha to come and stay with you next week?"

I stared. Had I actually *mentioned* that idea to her?

"Your father said you were thinking about it."

That's right. Dad and I did discuss it. During the same conversation in which I complained about not going to Toronto and he asked about my friend Hannah. I was about to snap back that Sasha and I weren't even talking to each other, in case she hadn't noticed, but I thought better of it.

"I haven't asked her. We haven't been hanging out much lately."

"Have you two had a fight?"

I was reading the entertainment section of the newspaper. A young, locally born pop singer rose to fame this month. I turned her winning smile face-down and looked at Mom. It unnerved me to see her eyes focused on me. Normally, she's lifting her head from a book, dreamy-eyed, and gazing at some point past my shoulder. She uses books the way some people use illicit substances. Is there a support group for that? *Hi, my name is Denise and I'm a recovering bookworm.*

Maybe she *is* recovering. I suppose a month of nonstop reading might make even the most hardened addict wonder if there's any more to life. Either way, I sensed Mom might actually be able to hear me today, so I said, "Sort of."

"Do you want to talk about it?"

"I don't know." I wasn't about to rehash it, especially since Mom didn't even remember the Gina Incident. "I think her family's going through kind of a ... rough patch."

"She could probably use a friend right now, then."

"You think I should invite her to stay here?"

"I don't want you staying here by yourself. But it might be fun for you and Sasha to be independent for a week, don't you think? You could buy groceries and experiment in the kitchen and ... play your music. I would phone every day. Of course, you're welcome to come to the cabin too. Marine said, 'Be sure to tell Natalie she's welcome.' I just don't want you to be bored."

Meaning, *cranky.*

So, it has got me thinking: maybe it's time I made a real effort to heal the rift with Sasha. I *did* go behind her back to date Kevin. Worse, I stopped calling her.

Speaking of Kevin ... I still fantasize about him, but three weeks have passed since our trip to the lake. The last time I saw him, we were cycling in the dark, and that was already two weeks ago. The intensity of his image is fading a bit. Maybe he has even left town.

Later

Called Sasha. Her voice sounded guarded. I kept things light and asked if she wanted to go to the beach tomorrow. She said she couldn't. (What's she doing all day, scrubbing the floors?) She hesitated a bit and then said, "You can stay over tomorrow night if you want. No one will be here." *Where is everyone?* I wanted to ask, but I couldn't: prying would make her angry. These days, the slightest thing sets her off. I just wish I understood why.

Friday, July 30th

The horror. I can't think about it yet. I'm too shocked to sleep. My legs twitch from all the walking. I've had one charley-horse already. I'm going to toss and turn all night. Maybe some music.

Saturday, July 31, 11:00 a.m., beach

I'm sitting on a log, my sandals kicked off. I crunch and release my toes and burrow them into the sand until I hit the wet stuff. I trace patterns on the slate of wet sand until I have to move to another log to find a smooth surface again. I'm hoping that focusing on my feet will lead to peace.

But it's not working. I'm still in shock. There's only so much I can take.

3:00 p.m., Con Brio

Came here seeking refuge. Lisa isn't here, and neither is Petra, but this place reminds me of them and their support. I've ordered a bowl of soup and a panini (I hope that's Italian for sandwich). I'm going to review the whole weird story. I certainly can't go home until I have.

So, Part 1: Sasha's Place

As planned, I arrived at 6 p.m. with a change of clothes and a toothbrush in my knapsack. When I rang the bell, Mrs. V. opened the door, wearing a tracksuit. Her bloodshot eyes and blotchy face made me flinch. She slurred her words. "Whadisit? Are you the paperboy? Come to get paid? Where's the paper? Can't get paid if you don't bring the paper!" She squawked a laugh. She was clutching a tumbler of amber liquid and ice cubes. When she saw me looking at it, she thrust it up in a toast. A bit of Scotch (?) sloshed over the side and I smelled alcohol. "Cheers, Natalie!" So she had recognized me.

A lit cigarette hung from her other hand. I've suspected for years that Sasha's mom smoked—underneath her Estée Lauder perfume, her pores exude the stale smell that I've noticed on other smokers. But I'd never actually caught her in the act.

She sucked hard on the cigarette and squinted. She shifted her weight unsteadily and leaned on the door frame. She looked at me over the rim of the glass and her eyes sparkled. Something funny hung in the air, and despite myself, I started to return her smile.

"So whatcha doin', Nat? Sniffin' around for my son like a bitch in heat?" She raised the tumbler and sipped.

The words stunned me. I couldn't move.

From behind her came an outraged cry. "You are *not* my mother! Get out of my way, you stupid drunk!" Sasha shoved past her mother and slammed the door.

The door opened as Sasha pulled me down the steps. "If you're not my daughter, I guess you won't be getting free room and board here anymore." She called Sasha an ungrateful bitch.

We walked. As if with one mind, we fell into step with each

other. We walked in silence; no words were necessary, or possible. We walked together; separating was unthinkable. We walked to the water because it was the only place to go. We walked until we were tired and then we sat on the beach and watched the surf.

After a long time, Sasha found a stick—half bat, half paddle. She collected stones the size of golf balls and stood at the water's edge. She threw them up and hit them one by one. She swung so hard I worried for her shoulder. Eventually, the stick snapped in two, and she flung the bottom half out to sea. It twirled like a propeller, fast as it rose, lazily as it sunk and then smacked the water. She turned and approached me, studying her palms. She looked up and shrugged. "Splinters."

I fought an impulse to touch her fingers and kiss them better. Memories were falling into place. When Sasha and I used to hang out in her room and her mother called us from downstairs, she yelled louder than she had to, sounding harsh and annoyed. When I phoned on weekend mornings, Sasha often said she couldn't talk to me because her mother was sick. A couple of times lately, Mrs. V. sounded vague and slurry on the phone, and later on, Sasha said she didn't get the message.

This is the twenty-first century and I know about alcoholism. As the Health teacher said, it's an illness, people are biologically predisposed towards it, it's not their fault, it needs to be managed, you go to AA, take medication, etc. etc.

But this was *my best friend's mother*.

"How 'bout pizza?" I said.

"Pacific Rim?" Sasha raised her eyebrows with the hint of a grin. Pacific Rim pizza was downtown. Our mothers didn't like us to go downtown by ourselves at the best of times, but they forbade us to go without telling them. *Our mothers.*

"You're on," I said.

We widened our strides and swung our arms.

As we ate slices of artichoke-heart and sun-dried-tomato pizza, Sasha filled me in. Her mom has always been an alcoholic, but she managed to stay sober for years at a time when Sasha and Kevin were growing up. Lately, she has relapsed more and more. She has sold hardly any houses for months. Her dad wants to move out but can't afford to support two households and doesn't want to just abandon her mom.

Kevin got caught in the crossfire. When he started partying—just the ordinary teenage stuff—fights happened. Their dad came home and found Kevin and his mom drinking together a couple of times. Bottles were poured down the sink, glasses smashed against the wall. Kevin got blamed for their mom's relapse. Now he couch surfs.

Only crusts remained on our plates. "And what about me? I can't keep living there with her ragging on me all the time. You heard her! She was supposed to go to my aunt's for a few days and give me some peace, but my aunt won't even talk to my mom if she's been drinking."

"You can stay at my house tonight." I dabbed a napkin at my mouth to soak up the grease.

Sasha stared over my shoulder so long that I turned to see what she was looking at. There was nothing there but a blurry painting of a lighthouse in a storm. She blinked and said, "It's okay."

"Are you sure? My mom really won't mind."

"She'll be passed out by now. I should go check on her. Make sure she's not choking to death on her own vomit or something." She checked to see how I'd reacted to that last comment. "I'm kidding," she said. Her bitter tone made it hard to believe she was joking.

We paid the bill and I walked Sasha home. The night hugged us, a dark cocoon. We turned off the main drag to escape the exhaust fumes. Wild roses scented the air. I ran my hands up and down my bare arms, chafing cool, goose-pimply skin. I hugged Sasha with one arm. We were alive, we were breathing, and that was all that mattered for now.

We reached the row of town houses where Sasha lived. "Do you want me to come in?"

She shook her head. "I'm used to it. It's no big deal."

"Are you sure? Why don't I just come in for a bit?" I started to move past her and up the cement path to their unit. She grabbed my upper arm and held it with a grip so strong, it made me suck in my breath.

Sasha stuttered in a husky whisper, "I don't … want you … to see her."

My stomach clenched. Slowly, I pried her fingers off my bicep. "Okay, Sash, I won't."

There were no lights on in the town house. I waited until she made it inside and then, with a caved-in chest, turned and began the trek home.

9:00 p.m., curled up on my bed
I couldn't face writing about Part 2 in Con Brio. I just wanted to be in my room.

Mom made chili and we ate together in silence. She peered at me to see what was wrong, but she doesn't suspect anything. She obviously doesn't know I saw.

jodi lundgren

Part 2: Our Place

My legs were burning by the time I arrived home. I noticed Marine's blue Honda in the driveway. A light glowed in the living room. Mom and Marine were probably watching a video. At the side of the house, jets of water were arcing and falling, arcing and falling. Mom had forgotten to turn off the sprinkler and the grass was soaked. A rivulet of water streamed down the curb, wasting itself in the street. To reach the faucet, I had to pass the living room window. I glanced inside and froze.

My mother and Marine were embracing on the couch. Marine's back was to me and my mother's hands were gripping it. Their faces were joined and they were twisting and turning their heads as if they couldn't get enough of each other's mouth but wanted to dig deeper, get under something. *Tongue wrestling, tonsil hockey, sucking face* … Kevin. I'd never seen Mom and Dad kiss like that. Mom pulled away and looked past Marine's shoulder right at me. She looked flushed and dreamy. I sprang back, afraid that she saw me, but I'm pretty sure all she could see was her own reflection.

Or maybe she had a moment of mother's intuition and knew one of her kids was suffering. Because I was. Suffering. I collapsed on the grass and soaked the seat of my jeans. The sprinkler continued to arc and fall, arc and fall; it traced feathers of water over my body on each pass until I was drenched. Despite the warmth of the night, I shivered and my teeth chattered. I had to get up. And since I had nowhere else to go, I went inside.

In the bathroom, I peeled off my wet clothes and turned on the shower. Steam rose as water pelted the stall. They would hear me and have a chance to compose themselves. I dried off and crawled into bed. Sure enough, Mom tapped on my bedroom door.

"Are you all right?"

"Yes." I didn't attempt to disguise my mood.

"Can I come in?"

"I'm trying to get to sleep."

"I thought you were spending the night at Sasha's."

I'd totally forgotten. Mom thought she had the house to herself tonight. I softened my voice a little. "Sasha's mom was sick, so they weren't up for having me stay over after all."

"Oh." She sounded disappointed. She obviously wanted to spend the night with Marine, and now that I had returned, Marine was going to have to leave. Well, tough! I *live* here. What am I supposed to do, go couch surf like Kevin because I'm in the way? Fuck that.

"'Night, Mom."

"Good night."

I switched off my light but tossed and turned as my quads and calves threatened to cramp. I'd just dozed off when an engine revved in the driveway. *Good night, Marine.*

This morning I acted like nothing happened. I'm walking around under a veil. This must be what they call denial. It means things are too screwed up to deal with so you pretend they never happened, that you didn't notice. You gloss over the facts with little half-truths like "Sasha's mom was sick." You avoid looking each other in the eye because you're both hiding what you know. It deadens you. Layers of something like gel separate us. All we're left with are secrets and shame.

Sunday, August 1st

When I joined her in the kitchen this morning, Mom announced that she had just called Sasha's house to talk to her mom about Sasha staying with me. That was bad enough, but then she explained that Kevin had answered. "He sounded like a very nice young man."

Kevin? The kicked-out Kevin was at home answering the phone? "What did you tell him?"

"I asked him if I could speak to one of his parents. He said his mom was visiting her sister and might be away for a few days. He wasn't sure where his dad was."

"Then what?"

"I said that Sasha was invited to stay with you this coming week while I'm away."

Does she know what she has done? Informed a homeless sexual predator that her fifteen-year-old daughter will be home alone for a week?

"He said he'd be sure to pass the message on, but that he didn't see a problem. He said he would keep an eye out for you girls."

"How nice of him."

She registered my sarcasm. "Natalie, I think he recognizes that he's too old for you. I mean, it's been a month since he asked you to the fireworks, and he hasn't asked you out again, right? I really got a good feeling from him."

I wanted to blurt out everything to let her know how clueless she really is, but my mouth felt dry. What was there to say, really?

I never did invite Sasha to stay here. Mom just assumes I have. She's obviously desperate to be alone with Marine, or she wouldn't be so hasty. Fine. I won't burst her horny little middle-aged bubble. I guess it's about time she got laid. Who knew, though? Who *knew* this was the reason she never showed interest in men after she and Dad split up? God. Wouldn't Dad be shocked? Or does he know? Does he *know* and is that one of the reasons they got divorced?? I'm going to go insane if I don't get my mind off this.

Night

Mom came into my room just now to reassure me that I'm welcome to join her and Marine if I don't feel comfortable staying here. Or at any point during the week, to just call and they'll come pick me up, even though it's a three-hour drive. She doesn't mean it, though. I can tell. She wants time alone with her *lover*.

I haven't felt this unwanted in as long as I can remember. Even Paige hasn't returned my call, and it has been two days. I suppose she is having the time of her life with Dad and Vi—that Dad has made this the year he finally learns how to take a vacation. Go, Dad.

Monday, August 2nd, 11:00 pm.

I spent some time snooping as soon as Mom left for the cabin. In the drawer under her bed, I discovered a small set of books with words like "lesbian" or "coming out" in the title. One was called *Gay Parenting*. Does that mean Mom isn't the only one? How reassuring. I slammed the drawer shut.

The fridge paid better dividends. I found a carton of Chocolate Chip Cookie Dough ice cream at the back of the freezer and planted myself in front of the TV. I spooned it straight from the carton as I flipped channels, in a trance, numb. When the phone rang, I ignored it.

The pit of my stomach rebelled. I glanced down to find the carton three-quarters empty. I ran to the bathroom and sat on the toilet as my bowels rumbled and fussed. Diarrhea, sort of. I felt sick to my stomach and my head swam. I'm still spinning out on sugar now.

Abusing food isn't that much fun. How 'bout another vice?

Tuesday, August 3rd
You must have been expecting me.
Did you miss me?
I stayed away as long as I could.

He arrived on the doorstep tonight with Chinese take-out and white wine. Five-o'clock shadow didn't hide the dimple in his cheek. My guts churned. They always churn when I see him. He makes me feel.

Friday, August 6th
hope floats
trees finger the sky
waves lap the dock
smoke in my throat
heat in my belly
a hand between my thighs

relaxed at last
warmth spreads

do it again

This week is a stolen jewel. We don't answer the phone. Mom calls once a day and I return her call when things are quiet and I'm sober. Kevin shops with the money she left for groceries, and we borrow his friend's car to get to the lake. That's what the poem is about. Kevin says it reminds him of haiku. I got stoned for the first time—Kevin brought weed—and now we do it every day. We sleep in the nude in Mom's double bed. We haven't gone all the way, but we, how should I put this, pleasure each other. Pretty much all we do is drink and smoke weed and laugh and fool around. Kevin answers the door for the pizza guy with a towel wrapped around his waist. One time I heard a woman's voice at the door. He came back without pizza. "What happened?" I asked. He looked embarrassed. "I must have scared her off!" When the doorbell rang again, it was a man.

I've discovered I have a strong sex drive. What I mean is, I feel all tingly and hot below the waist most of the time. It's delicious. Kevin is dying to go further but he doesn't pressure me. I'm not ready. I'm discovering all these new sensations. Like tickling, but better. So much better.

Night

Kevin and I snuggled on the couch as we watched *Spinal Tap*. I haven't done that in years! Mom stopped cuddling with me, or maybe I stopped wanting to cuddle with her, when I was about eleven. We barely even hug anymore. I forgot how *good* it feels. We didn't drink or smoke or make out. We were both tired and content to just sit there. *I think I'm falling in love with him!*

Saturday, August 7th

According to Kevin, we're broke. He asked if I could get more money from Mom and that made me mad. I know she left enough to last a week but if we've gone through it on "extras," then that's not her responsibility. Mom isn't there to support Kevin's habits. He got pissed off and left. I'm going to spend the afternoon cleaning up this pigsty. Things have gotten out of hand in the past few days. We've left pizza boxes and dirty plates and wet towels all over the house.

Sunday, August 8th, 2:30 a.m., post party

Party, property damage, police.

> And not only that.
>
> What have I *done*?
>
> I'm going to take a bath.

9 a.m.

Mom will be here by noon. It seems like she called just after I'd drifted off to sleep. The owners of the resort had woken her up at 8 a.m., frantic, saying the police were on the line. So these are my last few hours of independence. It's probably just as well.

Yesterday, Kevin came back to find the house cleaned up and called me Martha Stewart. I said maybe he needed to find another couch to surf. The honeymoon was definitely over.

He told me he wanted to have some friends over. I didn't think it was a good idea.

We argued about it for a long time and then we made up because he came up behind me, nuzzled my neck, and slid his arms around my waist. My knees practically buckled. I twined my arms around his neck, he sucked my earlobe, and we ended up in the bedroom again. The sun slanted across the bed, and after the fight I felt extra emotional. We were both sober. He looked into my eyes, and, well …

Afterwards, I still didn't want him to have the party. He said it was too late, his friends were already coming over, but not to worry, they were all mellow.

I worried. I tried to party-proof the whole house by hiding valuables and breakables. I piled dining room chairs on the stairs to block off the top floor. Kevin thought I was overreacting. The one thing we agreed on was that everyone would smoke outside. People are used to that, anyway, Kevin said. Smokers like to hang outside, especially on beautiful August nights.

I dressed up a bit and put on makeup before the party so I'd look older. Kevin said I looked sexy and sixteen and a half at least. When his friends showed up, he presented me with a six-pack of citrus coolers. He said I was a good sport about drinking beer, but he knew girls liked girl drinks and these were all mine. I kissed him on the cheek in front of his friends.

The stoners really were pretty mellow, though I was nervous the smell of weed would carry to the neighbors' yard. I refused to toke, wanted to stay clear. When the three guys from The Ice Cream Place parking lot showed up—good old Tyler, Steve, and Brad—things got a little rowdier. They changed the music to heavy metal and had beer-chugging contests in the living room. I don't think they recognized me. They didn't make any pedophile jokes, anyway.

But apparently Tyler invited the whole Canwest soccer team. Even Kevin got nervous when he heard that. Once the team started streaming in, half of them still in their red-and-white tracksuits, all we heard about was the game. They had won, but with controversy. One of them had body-checked an opponent without being penalized, and the other side resented the victory. The Canwest players themselves were divided about the call. The body-checking teammate didn't even come to the party. The few girls who came weren't very friendly. One of them, named Vanessa, warmed up a little bit when I complimented her auburn and blonde streaked hair. (I didn't mention that she could be the Canwest mascot: red and white!)

Then tires were squealing out front; the other team showed up looking for a fight. People swarmed the lawn. Someone threw the first punch, and a rumble broke out. They snapped a sapling in half and trampled flowerbeds. By the time the police showed up, most people had scattered. The place was strewn with beer bottles. The stoners slipped out back and down the alley with their stash just in time.

Kevin vanished.

I faced the police alone as a few remaining partiers gathered their things and left.

When the cops questioned me, I fell apart. I blubbered and couldn't get words out. They finally called Mom's resort, but she was in a cabin with no phone and the main office was closed. They couldn't reach her. They called Dad in Oakville and left a message. His cell phone was turned off (he's obviously taking this vacation stuff seriously now), and I've lost the number for Vi's family cabin, if that's where they are. They asked me who my local guardian was. I thought of telling them: Kevin Varkosky.

After all, he's nineteen: legally an adult.

I overheard the cops talking about calling the detachment in

Parksville and getting them to send someone out to Mom's cabin, but when I pictured an officer banging on the door and surprising Mom and Marine in bed, I pulled myself together. "Please don't disturb my mother in the middle of the night. I'll be fine on my own. Really." They said they'd follow up in the morning.

Mom's on her way. What do I tell her?

There's stuff I can't think about.

Night

I stripped the sheets from Mom's bed just before she arrived. No time to do laundry. A couple of Kevin's dark hairs clung to a pillow. I pulled off the case, the size of my torso, and held it in front of me. Fists level with my heart, I yanked hard, tearing fabric to my abdomen, making rags from where his head had lain.

She pulled into the drive in her green Volvo just before noon. I opened the front door and waited. Kermit's engine rumbled and sputtered before it died down. Mom lumbered out of the car as if she had forty extra pounds strapped to her back. I'd never seen her look so old. She hadn't combed her hair and when she pushed her sunglasses up, her eyes had sunk in their sockets. Marine wasn't with her and I was glad.

She reached the porch and I stayed in the door. "Natalie, what happened?"

"Sasha's brother threw a party here last night."

She hung her head. "Was anyone hurt?"

I joined her in looking at the door mat. "No."

"Thank God!"

She flung herself at me and scooped me into a hug. I let her hold me for a little while but then I started thinking about Kevin and Marine and it felt gross and confusing. I pushed her away.

"I'm sorry if I gave you too much responsibility. I forget that you're still just a kid sometimes."

"I am NOT a kid!" I shouted.

"No, well, I mean, a teenager."

"I'm a WOMAN!"

Mom just looked at me. I burst into tears. I could tell she wanted to comfort me but was scared to touch me again. "Let's go inside," she said. She led the way to the kitchen and we sat facing each other at the table.

"Did anything happen that you want to tell me about?" she said at last.

"No!" I shouted. I kept sobbing.

Mom made some chamomile tea. She boiled the water, scalded the pot, and set the cups in their saucers as I wept. Seeing as she wasn't asking me any more questions, I calmed down and pulled a cup towards me. She patted my hand. It was like she knew, she instinctively knew, and she sympathized.

I was thinking of telling her what happened with Kevin when an image flashed of her and Marine kissing. She doesn't *deserve* to hear my secrets, she hasn't *earned* them. She keeps secrets from me. I scowled and snatched my hand away. I wanted to say that I hoped she and Marine had lots of "adult fun" at the cabin.

"It's the garden!" I said finally. "They wrecked the garden."

Mom hurried outside. Images of the snapped sapling and trampled pansies looped in my mind as my shoulders shook and tears landed in my tea.

She stayed out there long enough for me to get the first round of sobs out of my system. The phone rang until the machine picked up. "Denise? Natalie? Are you there? I just received a message from the Victoria police and I want to know what the hell is going on." Dad paused and softened his voice. "I mean, I want to know if everything is all right. I'm going to call the police in ten minutes if I haven't heard back from you. Please call me."

The front door opened and closed. Mom shuffled into the hallway and took her time getting back to the kitchen. She was stooping. I blew my nose and told her she had better call Dad. Serves him right if he feels helpless and worried when shit happens, living that far away.

I've got to call Lisa.

Monday, August 9th

A book lay open on Mom's lap as I passed the living room, but she was leaning back in her armchair and staring into space.

I rolled my eyes. "Good book, Mom?"

She blinked rapidly several times. "I can't seem to focus, actually."

"Wonder why," I said under my breath.

Now she's unloading the dishwasher, folding laundry, and bundling the recycling. She does domestic chores when she's upset, so the sound of her bustling always unsettles me. Especially tonight.

I'm huddled as small as possible on this single mattress. I'm trying to compress my spirit, like a tightly-packed snowball. I want to shrink, to take up as little space as possible. Can a person will her uterus to contract? How much muscular control do we have over our internal organs, how tight can we squeeze them?

Listen here: anyone trying to find mooring in there, forget it. There's no room at this pier. Keep floating until it's time to leave.

God, this is exhausting. My muscles clench like this when

I'm cold, as if trying to keep the heat in. I feel cold right now. Peppermint tea?

Made myself a cup of tea in the kitchen. Mom wandered in and asked me if I'd been on the phone. I snapped at her that I hadn't. She picked up the kitchen phone to check for a dial tone. She looked so sad when she realized that, yes, of course the phone was working. It just wasn't ringing. She's so transparent. I should have offered her some tea, but there was only one bag of peppermint left, and frankly, I wasn't in the mood to share. Now she's watering the garden.

Peppermint smells so clean.

I'm still stiff with worry.

Before, I glossed over what happened the afternoon of the party. I want to get it out, I want the relief.

Fighting had stoked our emotions. We hadn't made out for almost two days after doing it nonstop. We hadn't drunk or smoked weed. Kevin's touch alone made me high. I felt an urge to get even closer to him. I could tell he felt it too. He was *there*, more present than ever, really seeing me. He raised himself on his elbows and looked down—half-smiling, half-questioning. I gazed back. Nothing was said. He started pressing himself between my legs. At first it felt good. Then he started thrusting, like he was hammering at a locked door, and I got scared. My muscles tensed and it hurt. He said, "Just relax." I was about to say "Stop" when something gave. He pushed in and came to rest, as if, after all that struggle, he had found a hold. And I held him.

He groaned and pushed more, in and out, sliding deeper each time.

I was getting alarmed. "Kevin!"

He didn't respond. His eyes were closed, lips apart, as he pumped. Finally he swore, "Oh, God, oh, Jesus." He yanked away and liquid spread over my stomach and thighs. He rolled onto his back as I sat up. Semen glistened on my belly.

"Don't worry, babe, I was careful."

It stung between my legs. I patted my stomach and thighs with a sheet.

"Lie back down and cuddle with me," he said. It came out as a whine.

I balled up the soiled sheet and carried it to the laundry hamper.

He was "careful."

But how does he *know?*

Tuesday, August 10th

I called Lisa's house and her mom answered. She was proud of her daughter for landing a job at an insurance company (as an "administrative assistant"). I agreed that it was hard to get any kind of office work right out of high school. I admitted that it wasn't simply luck; Lisa deserved it. I couldn't comment on the organizational skills Lisa displayed as a toddler, but I seconded the idea that landing this job boded well for her entire career.

In other words, I said "Uh-huh" for what seemed like an hour. When I finally pried Lisa's work number out of her mom, I called and asked to see her as soon as possible. We met at her office at four-thirty.

We walked down to the Inner Harbour and found an empty bench. Sailboats bobbed and chimed in front of us. I kept my eyes on the wharf as I told my story. Halfway through, I remembered our heart-to-heart back at Con Brio in July. My concerns were so immature back then—*Sasha's not speaking to me because I went to the fireworks with her brother.* I wished I could reverse time! I don't know what I expected Lisa to do about my current problem. She said nothing until I was finished. Perched on a wooden post, a seagull was crying in rhythmic repetition, its beak open wide.

"When exactly did this happen?"

"Saturday afternoon."

Lisa counted on her fingers. "Then there's no time to waste. You can get Plan B at the drugstore, but you have to take it within seventy-two hours."

"Plan B?"

"The morning-after pill."

She led me to a small pharmacy close by. I hoped it would be more private than the big-box drugstore. As we pushed open the glass door, dusty, perfumed air engulfed us. We headed for the back. In the diaper aisle, a young woman bounced up and down, trying to soothe the infant strapped to her front and at the same time corral a runaway toddler. An elderly woman stood at the dispensary, leaning on a cane. The white-smocked pharmacist's assistant had to shout at her and I cringed, worried that she would shout when it was my turn, too, and announce my dilemma to everyone in the store.

The hard-of-hearing lady took a seat right next to the counter. So much for privacy. I was grateful my own grandmothers weren't around to overhear me right then. It wasn't my proudest moment.

Lisa nudged me and we both stepped forward. I kept my eyes on the counter and mumbled my request.

"Pardon?" The woman kept her voice raised, perhaps trying to model the appropriate volume.

I shot Lisa a pleading look, and she said, "My friend would like to talk to the pharmacist."

"I screen all the requests," the woman boomed.

"It's about Plan B," I said.

"You'll have to speak up."

My cheeks were burning. Other customers had lined up behind me. "Plan B!"

The assistant's expression instantly changed: I was one of *those* girls.

"Have a seat in the consulting booth. The pharmacist will be with you shortly."

Only one person could fit into the booth, which reminded me of the penalty box at an ice rink. I didn't want Lisa to leave. "You'll be fine." She squeezed my hand and smiled, flecks of amber glinting in her brown eyes. I nodded and shut myself in. Since the gate was only a few feet high, it didn't really serve any purpose. The walls, the counter, and the shelves were stark, hospital white. Fluorescent lights glared on all the surfaces and lit the vacant seat opposite me.

At last the pharmacist arrived, wearing a white crewneck shirt under his smock, kind of like a priest's collar. *Forgive me, father, for I have sinned.* He extended his arm and introduced himself. I had to stand up to shake his hand, which was dry and powdery. "How can I help you?"

Why do doctors and pharmacists always make you repeat to them what you've just told their assistant? At least I didn't have to shout, and Plan B was less embarrassing to say than morning-after pill.

"Were you using any birth control at the time?"

I shook my head and stared at my lap. *Would I be here if I'd been using birth control?* I pressed my knees together tight.

"When did you have intercourse?"

Oh my God! So much for skipping the embarrassing part. *Lisa, what have you done to me?* But it wasn't Lisa. It wasn't even Kevin. I had done this. I had to answer.

"Saturday."

Like Lisa, he counted back.

"Saturday night?"

What was he going to want to know next? The position, the duration, and the estimated time of ejaculation on the twenty-four-hour clock?

"Saturday afternoon."

"Saturday after*noon?*"

Yes, we're kinky, we do it in the daylight. Don't you wish you were young again?

"Plan B is only effective if taken within seventy-two hours of intercourse, so you're almost out of luck. I can help you out this time, but before I do, I'm obliged to give you some information about birth control."

He launched into the available options, emphasizing the effectiveness rate and pushing pamphlets across the counter to illustrate each method. Educators make sex sound like a dentist appointment, right down to the hygienic rubber gloves. They talk about "getting swept away in the moment" like it's a health risk and not the point of the whole experience. I can't help it: I want sex to be romantic.

At last he stopped talking and handed me two small paper cups: one held the pill, the other water. He watched me swallow and gave me a second pill to take twelve hours later. When he said, "How are you going to pay?" I stopped short. I honestly thought he meant *pay for your sins* until he placed his hand on the till. Fortunately, I had enough cash. I didn't want any record of the purchase on my bank statement.

I escaped from the booth, still blushing, and found Lisa browsing in the greeting card aisle. At least there wouldn't be any New Baby cards in my near future.

"Ready to go?" she said.

On the sidewalk, I took huge strides, distancing myself from the store as fast as possible. The air was cooling as evening approached.

"You look relieved. Embarrassed, but relieved."

"I am *never* going through that again! NEVER!"

Lisa giggled. "That's exactly how I felt a couple of years ago."

"You've been through that too?"

She dropped her eyes to the sidewalk, then looked at me. "How do you think I knew what to do?"

I shook my head. "I'm so lucky you were there. You have no idea ..."

It was five-thirty. Throngs of people were milling about. Some wore dress shirts and carried briefcases; some wore T-shirts and carried backpacks. But they all looked the same: used up and hungry for dinner. They clustered at bus stops, ear buds in place, and winced as if their shoes were too tight. Not me. I wanted to burst out singing.

Lisa was chewing her lip. "I hate to bring this up, but ..."

I froze to the spot. The stream of foot traffic parted around me. My good mood evaporated. "What is it?"

"There's one other thing you need to take care of."

She must be thinking of the second pill. "The pharmacist gave me another pill to take at home."

Lisa touched my shoulder. "Let's keep walking."

We turned off Douglas and onto View Street, where the crowds thinned out.

"It's not about Plan B. It's about STIs."

"STIs?" I thought she was referring to a TV show at first. But that's CSI. "Oh! You mean—"

We both said it together: "Sexually Transmitted Infections." I groaned.

"You don't have to go today." Lisa tried to make her voice sound reassuring. "The timing doesn't work quite the same way."

I wanted to punch a wall, but suddenly I was afraid to touch anything. The whole of downtown must be crawling with germs.

"Just Google the Sexual Health Clinic and call them to set up an appointment."

We were close to the Saint Vincent de Paul Society, where there's a soup kitchen. A man with piercing eyes and matted hair stormed past us. "Sluts." At least, I could have sworn that's what he said.

My legs started trembling. "I can't handle any more right now. I've got to go for a run. Burn off some tension. Want to come?"

Lisa gestured to her work clothes. "I can't, but you go ahead."

We parted, and I tore down the sidewalk, weaving through the rush-hour crowds and away, away, away from downtown.

Wednesday, August 11th

This morning Mom and I pulled on gardening gloves and armed ourselves with shovels and spades. We didn't say much. Like a search-and-rescue team, we replanted the flowers and shrubs we could save and piled up the ones we couldn't. The trunk of the ornamental cherry tree had split; sap oozed from the core and congealed. We'll have to go to the nursery if we want to replace it, but we didn't discuss it. I think we both need some time.

I did some mental sorting as we salvaged the garden. I wish I knew where Kevin was. I don't know if I want to talk to him right now, but I keep thinking about Saturday. If it weren't for the party, we would have had time to figure out what everything meant. We weren't drunk, and that seems important. I saw the way he looked at me—I know he feels something. But is it the same as what I feel? Am I his girlfriend? I saw him talking to that Vanessa girl just before the rumble broke out and everyone dispersed. Where did he spend the night? Where is he now? Four days have already passed.

Thursday, August 12th

My period was officially due last Sunday. Is Plan B guaranteed, or not? Maybe I'm really pregnant! What will I do? A baby would ruin my life, but so would an abortion. I can't have either one. But I would have to. Unless I killed myself. Or had a miscarriage—how common is that? I've heard Mom's friends talk in hushed voices about miscarriages like they cause horrible trauma. But I would give anything for that to happen to me right now.

The strange thing is, even though I know how much trouble it causes, I can't stop thinking about sex.

Lisa says that the muscle contractions involved in orgasm can trigger your period. That means there is something I can do. *Alone.*

Evening

It worked! I "induced" my period! I've never been so happy to see blood. Lovely dark red bodily fluid.

Friday, August 13th

It's Friday the thirteenth, but the blood still flows—I am blessed, not cursed. Or maybe a little of both. How can Kevin have just disappeared like this? It's almost like last week was a dream. What if I didn't know Lisa? *You know he got a girl pregnant last year, don't you?* Sasha's voice echoes in my head. Was she telling the truth? And if so, what became of that girl? Sasha surely would have mentioned a baby—a niece or a nephew, to her!

Mom just called out that she's running some errands. She never used to frame her plans so vaguely. No doubt it's a tip from *The Rules for Dating as a Single Parent*: "Don't burden your children with the details of your dating life, but never lie to them about it, either." Like I care. Honestly, I'm just glad she's giving me some time to myself so I don't always have to escape to the beach or Con Brio.

Just remembered, Lisa told me to call her. I hear Kermit's motor receding. Now's my chance.

Lisa was happy to hear the news. She was at the office, and I should have just left it at that. But I wanted to get her opinion on whether I should try to find Kevin. She said, "He knows where you are. He should be calling *you*. And not just because of what happened between the two of you. He had a party against your wishes in your mother's house and abandoned you to face the police. What kind of a person does that, Natalie? I really think you should forget him."

I've never heard Lisa sound so adamant. Usually, she sees all sides of a situation and doesn't pass judgment. I see her point, I really do. But acid is corroding my stomach lining, I want to see him so bad.

Lisa also asked me if I'd gone for my screening yet. My first thought was of some auditions Petra had told us about. But that's not what Lisa meant. "You know, at the clinic?"

I groaned. "Do I *have* to?" The last thing I needed was more people judging me with their looks the way the pharmacist's assistant had.

"I would if I were you." She paused. "I'll call and make an appointment for you, okay?"

I sighed. She obviously wasn't going to let this go. "Okay." I hung up, hoping to forget about it for another week or so.

But she called right back. "They had a cancellation. I got you in for Monday afternoon at one."

"Great," I said with zero enthusiasm.

Really. Can't wait.

Saturday, August 14th

The blood still pours—they never told me it would be an extra-strength period like this. It's kind of reassuring, though. The little zygote—if there is one—is sure to be flushed out. My energy has ebbed. I'm sitting in a deck chair trying to soak up some sun. Mom just asked if it's all right to have Marine over for dinner, and I pleaded that I wasn't feeling well enough to have company. As she listened, her face betrayed the same hunger that I'm feeling—a tapeworm eats away at her, too.

Just now Mom followed up with a second question: "Do you mind if I go out for dinner?"

I said, "Please do, that would be great," maybe too enthusiastically. I never thought I'd say this, but I can't wait to go back to school. Mom and I are crowding each other out.

Evening

Mom popped her head into my room on her way out. I detected an unfamiliar odor. "What's that smell?"

She blushed. "Do you mean my perfume? It's sandalwood. Don't you like it?"

"It's okay. Since when do you wear perfume?"

Mom cleared her throat. "It's something new I'm trying. Just for fun, now and then."

She assured me she wouldn't be out late. I think she doesn't want me to get any ideas about inviting guests over. As if!

It's my one-week anniversary of losing my virginity. I don't think I bled when it happened—my hymen must have been broken already by tampons and fingers. Or maybe even by doing high kicks and the splits.

So why is losing my virginity such a big deal, then? I don't know why, but it is. I had *someone else* inside my body! How weird is *that*? It's so confusing.

I really thought I was falling in love.

No.

I thought *we* were falling in love.

It has been a whole week. Has he forgotten me; has he hooked up with someone else—like Mascothead Vanessa? I'm sure I saw her gawking at him. Has she sunk her trendy little claws in him? Does he like her body better? Is she better in bed? Does he prefer someone older and more experienced?

OH MY GOD! I CAN'T STAND THIS! Maybe it's not too late to win him back, if I can only get hold of him.

Later

*67'ed the Varkoskys. Mrs. V. answered.

"May I speak to Kevin, please?" I pitched my voice higher to disguise it.

"Who is this?"

Panic silenced me.

"Is that you, Diane? I've asked you to stop calling here. Do you understand me? Kevin is dead as far as you're concerned."

A male voice sounded in the background just before the receiver clicked. Was it Kevin?

Who the hell is Diane? The pregnant girl? How many women has Kevin slept with? How many of them were virgins? Does he make a habit of seducing virgins and ditching them once they've given in? And does he always go after younger girls? Do women his own age see through him?

How could he disappear on me like this?

Sunday, August 15th

I set up a sleeping bag on the deck last night. Hard to believe it has been a month since Paige and I slept out there. The earth is passing through an asteroid belt. I kept a soft focus to my gaze because, at any moment, a star could fall anywhere in the dome above me. And did they ever. Long, comet-tailed streaks of light like matches being struck across the sky. Brief flicks like silver minnows darting in dark water. The meteors fell in an arc as they gave in to the earth's gravity. At times, they almost rained down. Silent cannon balls that burned up before they hit a target—thankfully!

I must have drifted off to sleep because the next thing I knew, the sliding glass door was screeching open, the patio light was switched on, and Mom was yelling, "Natalie!"

I rubbed my eyes. They felt sealed shut, and it stung to force them open. I squinted at the looming, backlit figure of my mother.

"Natalie!"

"Yes, I'm here, what is it?"

"My God! Why didn't you tell me?"

"Tell you what?"

"I came home and saw that you weren't in bed. I've been calling everyone! I've been frantic! Sasha's mother sounded drunk and said Kevin wasn't there and she hasn't seen him in days and she wouldn't give me the number where she thought he might be staying, so I tried directory assistance, but no luck. I called your dad and couldn't get him on his cell phone so then I was frantically searching for the number at the cabin and I couldn't remember how to spell Vi's last name—can you believe it? So I had to hunt for Paige's letters and finally found the one with the cabin phone number but of course it was the middle of the night out there and I woke everyone up. Your dad wasn't too pleased and said that there was nothing for it but to call the police. I hung up and called Marine, and even she thought it was the best thing to do, and coming from her, that's quite a statement because just between you and me she still calls them 'pigs' behind their back, she's got those old hippy values, not that I don't, I can see where she's coming from with that, but I think it's different when you don't have kids, when you have kids you're pretty grateful to have *some* kind of higher authority to turn to in an emergency—"

"Mom! Calm down!" She was freaking me out with her non-stop talking. I snuggled deeper into the sleeping bag.

She kept right on going. "I was still on the phone with Marine when call waiting popped up and I thought it was going to be Sasha's mom calling back to tell me where you and Kevin were but it was Paige. Paige had woken up, too, and wanted to know what all the fuss was about, and when they told her, she calmly said, 'Have you checked the balcony? Nat is probably sleeping under the stars.' And here you are."

"Correction: I *was* sleeping under the stars."

"You should have left me a note in the kitchen. I was worried sick."

"I'm sorry. I just never thought it would be a problem."

I traipsed back to my bedroom, then, because the sun rises awfully early at this time of year. It took me quite a while to get back to sleep after that tirade. Now I know how stressed out I've made my mother with the P&P (party and police) incident. I'm going to have to straighten up because I don't think she's too stable. I've never seen her talk a mile a minute like that. Maybe she's feeling especially fragile with everything that's going on in her own life these days. Everything she's still keeping in.

It's kind of funny that she's done some of the ground work. *I'm* dying to know where Kevin is too. Now I can scratch his mom and directory assistance off the list.

Evening

Mom and I have pretty much avoided each other all day. I've had a lot of time to think. I'm starting to come around to Lisa's perspective. It sucks that Kevin did what he did and then vanished. He knows where I am. He could have found me.

It hurts.

Monday, August 16th, morning

Am having a major mope fest. Tried Googling and 411ing Kevin and his tree-planting company—no results. Combed my memory for "Diane"—has Sasha ever mentioned her? Was that the name of the woman Kevin supposedly knocked up last year? Maybe she *did* keep the baby. Maybe Kevin is a father! If so, it's pretty cruel of Mrs. V. to cut off the mother of her own *grandchild!* Doesn't Kevin have a legal obligation to pay child support? Or maybe he denies it—maybe they're demanding proof of paternity, like on those talk shows where they make the guests argue for the whole show before they finally announce the results of a DNA test.

Mom just headed out again. Said she had to stop by the school. Yeah, sure. She'd fluffed up her hair and was wearing a new dress. The smell of sandalwood hung in the air. Her cheeks were pink from excitement, rather than makeup, I think. She has always pooh-poohed cosmetics. Unless … could she be a "lipstick lesbian"? That might explain her new interest in perfume. Guys at school talk about lipstick lesbians: They watch them on those porn sites with free video clips. I'm not sure if they exist in real life, though. It didn't come up in Health class.

Should I raid the fridge to get my mind off all this? Mom would lose herself in a book.

Phone—saved!

Later

That was Petra!

She's participating in a choreographers' festival in Vancouver. It takes place the weekend after next. She hired professionals to remount the piece she set on our summer school, but one of them twisted her ankle and has to pull out. Petra was panicking, not sure if she could get anyone to learn it in time, when she remembered me.

She has invited me to perform!

I am going to dance professionally in Vancouver!

I don't think it's an exaggeration to say that this is the BEST THING that has ever happened to me at the BEST POSSIBLE TIME.

I've got to do laundry and pack. And go to that *stupid* appointment. I leave tomorrow morning—provided Mom approves, of course. But she will. It'll be good for both of us.

Monday night

Holy crap. That *sucked*.

Lisa said the testing wouldn't be too bad, but I think she forgot that I'd never had a pelvic exam before. Why would I? I wasn't "sexually active." And I'm still not. I don't think one time counts as "active." Like, if you do *one* long distance run *one* time and then stop working out completely, I don't think you can honestly call yourself "physically active." So why should it be different for sex?

The clinic was about a thousand times worse than the drugstore. I got lectured at both places, but at least in the drugstore I got to keep my clothes on. At least there, I didn't have to lie back, naked except for a scratchy paper sheet, my feet in stirrups like I was about to give birth. At least there, no one stuck things inside me—something big and plastic, like a water gun; something dry and wooden, like a Popsicle stick; something that wasn't a thing at all, but gloved and lubed *fingers*. I yelped. The doctor—and, oh yeah, it was a *male* doctor—kept telling me to relax in a crooning voice that I found *totally creepy*. A female assistant was looking on. That was supposed to make me feel more comfortable, but it didn't help one bit.

When the two of them finally ran out of things to do, they left the room to let me get dressed. It felt goopy where the lube had been. I should have wiped with a tissue from the box the woman waved at me, but I was in too much of a hurry to cover up. I thought I could split, but there was more. The woman came back, tied a tourniquet around my arm, and told me to make a fist. She said, "You might want to look away," but I watched. She stuck a needle in my elbow and filled up two vials with my blood. It made me feel queasy and light-headed.

As I staggered out, the receptionist stopped me. She wanted to know where to send the results, so that was another problem. I had to call Lisa at work. Luckily, the lady at the clinic said it was okay to send the results to Lisa's place.

"We'll see you next year." Her voice was chirpy, like a hostess at The Keg.

I just stared at her. *No, you WON'T*.

But I glanced at the pamphlets they'd loaded me up with as I walked home. I read that sometimes the infections won't show up in tests until months later. Also, once you've become "sexually active," you should keep having a pelvic exam *every year, even if you stop having sex!*

I threw the pamphlets away in a street-corner garbage can.

So here I am. Presumed healthy until proven infected.

Tuesday, August 17th

I'm sprawled on a life jacket container on the upper deck. The
sun is shining and tourists stroll past. They snap photos and point
at the islands. The ocean stretches blue and choppy on all sides.
Otters dive and seagulls ride the ferry's backdraft. The wind lifts
my hair, and the sleeves of my jacket ripple and snap like flags.
Every so often I see a dark-haired, lanky guy, and my body tenses.
I'm looking for Kevin everywhere.

A girl about my age is standing at the edge of the deck,
forearms propped on the railing. Her shoulder blades wing out
of her back like Sasha's. I guess it makes sense that I would see
her everywhere too.

The girl just turned her head in the direction of Victoria
and scowled.

It *is* Sasha!

Later

When I realized that Sasha was on the ferry, I zigzagged through
passengers to her side. "Hey."

She wouldn't look at me. She held the side of the ship and
I stood beside her, facing the scenery. Others lined the railing,
laughing and talking. The two of us were trapped inside a bubble
of tension.

"Why don't you just leave me alone?" Sasha clenched her jaw.

My arms pulled tight against my ribs as if I'd been shoved.
I took a few breaths before speaking. "I don't want to leave you."

We stood in silence as the Gulf Islands unspooled before us:
evergreens, cliffs of gray rock, and rust-colored arbutus trees that
reached for the water.

Sasha sniffed a few times and wiped her face with her sleeve.

I pretended not to notice she was crying. Her voice was hoarse and shaky when she finally spoke. "I'm running away. Things are totally out of control at home. Dad is trying to get Mom to go for treatment but there's a wait list. He's never home anymore. He sleeps in his office or stays in his friend's basement."

An image of Mrs. V. holding a tumbler of whiskey and swearing at Sasha from the front door came back to me. "So you're alone with your mom?"

She fixed me with her gaze for the first time that day. Mascara had smudged around her bloodshot eyes. Her punk-rock appearance matched her words. "It's fucking brutal."

Her dad is trying to get his own apartment for September first and wants Sasha to move in with him.

"Mom's threatening to kill herself. Like, she says, 'I might as well slit my wrists if you move out. I'll have nothing left to live for.'"

"Is she serious?"

"Does that sound like a *joke* you?"

"No, of course not." I bit my lips. Mrs. V. was way more messed up than I ever imagined. "Do you think she'd really do it?"

Sasha shrugged. "She's going to kill herself one way or another if she doesn't get some serious help."

It *sucks* to be fifteen! This has got to be the worst possible age in life. We have adult experiences, adult responsibilities, adult worries, but a kid's resources. We need support. We need role models. We need attention and love. Sometimes we even need supervision! But most adults can't even take care of themselves. They just give little kids the illusion that they're in control. At fifteen, you see through it and discover you're on your own.

"So what are *you* doing on the ferry by yourself? Getting

revenge because you didn't get to go to Toronto? Gee, Nat, life is rough."

I had to tell her about Petra's invitation.

"Aren't *you* the special one? I'd better be on my way. Don't want to drag the prima donna down with my problems."

I weathered her sarcasm. If there was ever a time not to take what she said personally, this was obviously it. I urged her to bus into downtown Vancouver with me. The thought of her wandering around by herself made me sick. We both knew that dealers and pimps lay in wait for girls like her. When she finally agreed to come with me, her face relaxed a bit. On the ride into town, her mood improved enough that she wanted to categorize the other passengers. The "blue-hairs" who ride the ferry free on weekdays and take the city bus to the mall. The neo-hippies with dreadlocks, mud-caked boots, and enormous backpacks who appear to have just left the bush after months of squatting, but who never actually leave the city limits. The mothers who struggle up the steps, block the aisle with strollers, and receive two kinds of stares: either, *Isn't that cute?* or, *Can't you make that baby stop screaming?*

At the bus stop, Petra looked startled to see two of us, but she invited Sasha to stay the night at her place. Petra lives with her boyfriend, Michel, who's away until the weekend. As soon as we arrived at their apartment—a character suite in a house with a bay window, an alcove kitchen, and a fire escape balcony—Sasha called her dad (at Petra's insistence) and worked it out: She'll stay here with Petra and me for the next three days while her dad arranges a place for them to stay. In the meantime, Sasha can take the warm-up class Petra gives to her dancers, watch rehearsals, and hang out with me. She also offered to poster for the show.

I hate to think of where she might have ended up tonight if I hadn't run into her. But it's freaking weird to be sleeping next to her on a blow-up mattress when not long ago I shared a bed with her *brother*! I haven't dared mention his name.

Wednesday, August 18th

This morning, Sasha and I pulled stools to the kitchen counter and ate breakfast while Petra made herself a sandwich. She offered to pack lunches for all of us, but, to save her trouble, I said that we wanted to try some of the local restaurants. It was sort of true. Since I discovered Con Brio, I enjoy eating out: It makes me feel older.

Petra caught me scraping my unfinished oatmeal into the garbage. "Didn't you like it?"

"It's not that—I'm just too nervous to eat!"

Petra snapped the lettuce container shut and stowed it in the fridge. "Don't be intimidated. Just use the rehearsal as a learning opportunity. I've got full confidence in your ability—and yours too, Sasha."

Sasha was reading the *Georgia Strait*. She grunted without looking up.

We bussed to the rehearsal hall on the edge of downtown. A skateboard shop with iron grids in all the windows occupied the ground floor. Petra stopped at the landing beside it and pulled open a heavy door. A long, narrow staircase led up to the second floor, where the studio awaited us.

Sasha said, "I don't think I'll take class, after all. I want to explore."

Panic surged in my chest. "Are you sure?"

I hoped Petra would encourage Sasha to stay, but she held

the door handle in silence. Judging by the concentration on her face, her mind was already in the studio. Sasha patted her backpack, which held a roll of packing tape and a stack of posters. "I'll hit some lampposts along the way." We arranged to meet on Robson later. I tried to send telepathic messages: *Stay out of trouble. Take care of yourself.*

Upstairs, a high-ceilinged, rectangular room with latticed windows and one mirrored wall formed the rehearsal space. The four other dancers were already stretching on the floor. Petra introduced me to Katrina, Halle, Beth, and Monique. They nodded and said, "Hi." Would I even remember their names? I followed Petra to a curtained alcove where we changed into our dance clothes.

"Ready?" she said.

"I hope so."

She touched my shoulder. "You'll do fine."

Petra launched into the warm-up class with no introduction. She kept up a fast pace and didn't give much feedback; she obviously wanted to warm up our bodies rather than actually instruct. The inside of my chest hollowed out. I really had to *work* to keep up with these *women*, these *professional dancers*. They looked so strong and moved with such power. I felt small and awkward in comparison.

My confidence trickled back when we ran the piece. I had already performed the dance and the others were still learning it. "Since you already know the material, think of enriching your movement," Petra said. She suggested that I watch the other dancers, look for qualities that I liked, and experiment with them. "Don't worry about copying them," she said. "It always looks different on another body."

After rehearsal, the others checked cell phone messages as they thrust arms into sleeves and pulled on pants. Everyone hurried except Monique, a petite twenty-two-year-old from Quebec, who asked me questions and chatted about herself. She finished a dance degree in Montreal just a few months ago, and she still feels a bit out of place in Vancouver. "It's tough coming to a new town, especially when it's not your culture," she said. We descended the stairs together, slowly. I liked to kick out my foot and let it hover in the air until gravity pulled me down and I sank to the next step, bending my knee like a spring. Monique noticed what I was doing and followed suit. "That makes me feel loose in my joints," she said. "Thank you, Natalie!" I like the way she says my name, which according to her is French. She puts equal stress on all three syllables: *Na-ta-lie*, and she really pronounces the *t.* In English, everyone says, *Na*-duh-lie.

When we reached the street, she checked her watch. "Oh, *mon Dieu*, I've got to run! I have to be at work. *À demain!*" The sidewalk was too crowded for running; she skipped and hopped to dodge people, and turned at the corner.

I still had half an hour, so I found a coffee shop and ordered a tuna melt. I needed to fortify myself before meeting Sasha. She probably wanted to check out the clothing stores on Robson Street. She likes to try on designer stuff and then buy second-hand clothes to mimic the style with her own twist. She should really look into fashion design as a career. I was making a mental note to suggest it when the waitress set my plate in front of me. Gooey orange cheddar dribbled over the sides of the open-faced Kaiser bun. A crisp dill pickle for garnish. My mouth watered. After skipping breakfast and dancing all morning, I was starved.

Later

At our meeting spot, Sasha grabbed my elbow and pulled me down the street. We walked for a few blocks without stopping. She showed no interest in any of the stores we passed. At the entrance to an office building, an alcove formed a haven from pedestrian traffic. She halted with her back to the street and opened her pack. "Look what I got!"

A silky dress, marked down to $120, in peacock blue and emerald green. The material slid under my hand and I longed to feel it swirl around my legs. "Gorgeous."

Sasha smiled and stuffed the dress into her backpack. That's when I noticed there was no store bag. I stiffened. "How did you afford this?"

"Boring question, Nat. You think it's gorgeous?"

"I said so. But … how did you pay for it?"

She rolled her eyes.

"Sasha, answer me."

She hummed to flaunt the fact that she was ignoring me.

"Did you steal it?"

"How would I steal it? You know the kinds of security systems they have in those places."

"You just answered my question with a question."

"You just answered my question with a question," she mocked.

"Listen, Sasha. I hooked you up with a place to stay in Vancouver. We're Petra's guests and there's no way I want her to be getting a call from the cops to come and bail you out for shoplifting!"

A passerby glanced in at us, startled, and Sasha glared at me. "Keep your voice down!"

She slung the bag over her shoulder and started walking. The Choreofest posters caught my eye in the outer pocket of her pack. She had no right to represent Petra. I hurried to keep up with her. She teetered on the curb at a red light, scanning oncoming traffic for a break, her chin jutted out. Steady traffic kept her from jaywalking. A cop car idled in the left turn lane.

We turned up a side street where the crowds thinned out. "Look, Nat, I'm sick of you playing all high and mighty with me. I know exactly what you've been up to this summer."

"What are you talking about?"

"Do I have to spell it out for you?"

"I'm afraid so."

We passed one sad, skinny tree after another, growing in squares of earth surrounded by pavement. The exhaust fumes made me feel nauseous.

"You've been fucking my brother."

I reeled as if punched in the gut. She kept walking but I veered to the cement wall of a building that bordered the sidewalk. I leaned my back against it and folded my arms across my chest. She turned around next to one of the skinny trees. We stared at each other. A showdown.

She shifted her weight and adjusted her backpack. Silence pulled taut between us. "Well? Are you going to deny it?"

She might have been bluffing. "What did he tell you?" My voice trembled. It was bad enough having her call me a slut way back in my previous life, when I was a virgin. This was too much to bear.

She strode up to me and stopped, hands on her hips, her dark bangs falling into her eyes. My old friend Sasha. "Remember the night you came over, the night I told you about my mom?"

"Um-hm."

"After that, I kept trying to call you. You never answered the phone. I needed someone to talk to, but I didn't feel like leaving messages."

Another blow. I'd forgotten Sasha. She shared her family secrets that night and never heard from me again. Some friend. "Sash, I'm so sorry."

She held up her hand. "I'm not done." She bit off her words and her eyes flashed.

"Later that week, I go over to your house. Your mom's car isn't there, so I ring the bell. I'm standing there waiting for you to answer the door, and I'm thinking how nice it'll be for you and me to reconnect. I'm feeling big enough to give you a second chance after you went behind my back to date my brother. I'm remembering how my mom swore at me in front of you that night, and how you didn't freak out. You just walked with me and listened and acted like a friend. I'm thinking nice thoughts about you, like how we've been friends for six years now, how we met in that skipping tournament on the playground, doing Double Dutch. I'm just about to ring the bell again when the door opens. My brother is standing there wearing nothing but a towel! Jesus, Natalie, how could you?"

She backed up a few paces and stared at the ground. I held my face in my hands.

She turned and continued walking. I trailed behind. When she reached a small park with grass, flower beds, and a statue of some explorer, she stopped. She sat down and grasped the bench, wrists flush with her legs. Her body curved forward into a tense cat arch. I joined her.

We sat together for awhile, looking at the rose garden, at the greenish statue of a man on a horse. "I'm sorry," I said. "I haven't been a good friend to you lately."

"You know what I don't get?"

"What?" For a second, it seemed that all our conflict stemmed from a simple misunderstanding. If she stated her confusion and I explained, we could shake hands and make up. Best friends forever.

"I don't understand how you can be such a bitch and a slut and still get whatever you want."

The words cut. They paralyzed me, especially the *s* word. It took something precious, filled it with hate, and bashed it. I had sex before I was ready, yes, and I've never seen Kevin again. That hurts. It hurts a lot. But to be judged and despised for what happened? The pain deepened with every breath.

After a long silence, I called up the image of Sasha crying on the ferry. It softened me enough to make one final effort. "Petra asking me to do this performance was my first lucky break all summer. Ms. Kelly kept ragging on me, remember? It was so bad that I dropped out of jazz. I really wanted to go with Paige to visit my dad, but they wouldn't let me. And my mom took off with her—" I caught myself just in time. This wasn't the moment to "out" my mother. "—her new *best friend*. They sure didn't want me around." There were my lonely ice-cream binges. "And—and lots of other stuff." Like losing my best friend, like losing my virginity. I swallowed hard.

Sasha sneered. "Never mind. I'll be gone in a couple days and we can forget this ever happened."

Our heart-to-heart was over. She took a winding route to a distant bus stop and I followed along. I suspected she was going out of her way to avoid the store she had stolen from. A heaviness settled inside my chest, worse than phlegm.

She kept the dress. She knows I won't say anything this time. And if there's a next time, I won't hear about it.

Thursday, August 19th

Petra pushed back our rehearsal time and urged us to take class at the Dance Centre. For the coming week, the guest teacher is Lance, the man Petra introduced me to after the show last month. She calls him her guru.

He stood at the studio entrance and greeted the dancers as we filed in. He stopped me and shook my hand. "Welcome! You're—" He half-shut his eyes as he tried to place me.

"Natalie."

"That's right—from Victoria." He smiled. "You're in town? Visiting?"

"I'm rehearsing with Petra for Choreofest."

He raised his thick gray eyebrows, pushing his forehead into deeper wrinkles. "How wonderful! I look forward to seeing you perform again. Have you taken a Graham-based technique class before? No? Then just find a spot in the center so you have people on all sides to watch."

At least twenty professional dancers surrounded me, a decent portion of them men. My neighbor to the left was six-feet tall and wore a wrestling singlet. Islanded in the middle, I followed as best I could. Class began on the floor, with contractions, releases, lifts, and leans. A live drummer made rhythm ricochet off the walls. We stood up for *tendues* and leg swings. The exercises progressed to combinations full of jumps that traveled diagonally, clear across the space. Lance encouraged and praised us all through the class. "Take the back with you. That's it. Open the chest around the heart. Beautiful!" His voice filled a hole inside.

After class, Lance said, "Congratulations, Natalie. You did very well your first time. How did you like it?"

"I feel like my spine's been through a wringer, but I loved it! There's so much more feeling in this kind of dance."

He placed his hand on his chest. "That's my goal: to teach you to dance from your emotional center. I want to make you feel safe enough to express what's in your hearts. With passion and accuracy." No teacher I'd ever met talked this way; even Petra wasn't quite so … *spiritual*.

I took a chance and said, "I feel really intimidated dancing with older people. I'm worried that Petra is disappointed in me. I think she must regret hiring me. I don't measure up."

Lance took a breath. "It was very brave of you to take on the challenge of performing professionally at such a young age."

Sure, if by "brave" he meant "foolhardy."

"You've had excellent training and your technique is strong. What it comes down to now is quality. Yes, it's going to take years to develop your full potential in modern." He spread his hands as if the future stretched between them.

"I knew it," I said. "But I don't have years, I have *days.*"

"I'm not finished." He clapped his hand on my shoulder.

I pursed my lips and scuffed my foot on the floor.

"All you need to do is open your heart," he said. "Let everything you're feeling spill into the dance. Even the doubts and fears. If you try to shut down your emotions, you'll look dry and academic." He swung his arms stiffly, like a soldier. "But if you welcome them in, you'll be convincing." He rolled his spine from side to side, contracted his stomach like he'd been punched, ran backwards, then turned and flung himself into a leap, legs and arms spread wide. He landed in a kneeling position and rolled back up to standing. He faced me. "You see?" He asked. "Make sense?"

I nodded. "I think so. I'll try my best."

He frowned. I was confused until I realized that he was mirroring my worried expression. It made me laugh. "That's better," he said.

He seems so wise and kind. I wonder if I could adopt him as my grandfather. I hardly remember Mom's dad—I was only four when he died—and my Ontario grandparents haven't flown out since the divorce.

Evening

Sasha didn't show at our meeting spot this afternoon. She'd gone "postering" again. I waited for fifteen minutes, then started strolling. After a few cool, overcast days, the return of hot weather had people parading by in sundresses, tank tops, shorts, and sandals. Bright colors and flowered patterns made a human garden that contrasted with the mannequins, already draped in darker autumn clothes.

A commotion across the street caught my eye.

Against a backdrop of giant faces—posters in a window display—a girl was running. The models pouted as she dodged and weaved, her long, dark hair and a pair of jeans streaming behind her. Sasha. In the doorway of the store, a clerk in a white T-shirt was jumping to see over the heads of the crowd. She called to another clerk who punched numbers into a phone. Sasha disappeared around the corner.

An elderly man with a canvas shopping bag in the crook of his elbow shuffled towards me. I veered to the right and a skateboarder loomed in front of me. He had a piercing in the middle of his lower lip, and round black discs stretched holes in his earlobes. He scowled as he rolled past.

I kept trying to dart through the crowd before I lost track of Sasha altogether. Finally, I rounded a corner.

"Why'd you sell my bedframe for drugs?"

I jerked to a standstill. Was someone yelling at me? A busker swung his guitar to face me. Shaggy blond curls fell over his forehead, and his eyes looked kind of sad. It was a line in a song he was singing, mostly on one note.

A passing business man bumped the neck of the guitar. "Don't block the sidewalk." As he strode by, he muttered, "Scum."

The busker kept right on playing. His strumming was fast and precise, like bluegrass music. He delivered the next line to the suit's back, raising the volume on the last word. *"Why'd you sell my bedframe for drugs—MOTHERFUCKER?"*

He looked down at the frets. His hands spanned the strings and his fingers quivered with strength. A guitar case lay open at his feet and a few golden coins dotted the black lining. I shoved my hand into my pocket as I glanced up the street. I'd lost Sasha's trail, anyway, so I took time to fish out a coin. Busking didn't look easy. When I dropped in some change, the musician nodded and flashed me a smile.

"Friends don't do that kind of stuff. Why'd you sell my bedframe for drugs?"

I turned back the way I'd come. I didn't know what to do about Sasha. (*"Why'd you pawn off my videos?"* the singer asked.) If I tried to talk to the store clerks, they might think I was an accomplice. They would definitely want me to help them catch her. I didn't want to cover for her, but I didn't want to turn her in. So I did nothing.

Tonight, Sasha's dad called Petra to say that he had come to Vancouver and picked Sasha up and could Petra please send her things home with me next week. He didn't explain why he was a day early or why Sasha had left her stuff. So I don't know if she was arrested, or if she just freaked out and called her dad. Petra asked me if I knew what had happened, and I shook my head.

I didn't used to have all these secrets. It makes me feel tired and old.

Friday, August 20th

This morning in rehearsal, Petra said we were coming across as ethereal and weightless, like good ballerinas. But she wanted us to be grounded and earthy.

My shoulders tightened when I heard the criticism. I assumed it was directed at me. I'm the one with the least experience in modern dance, after all. Practically none. I was probably bringing down the level of the group. Isn't that what Ms. Kelly said when she kicked me out of the jazz piece? My God, what was I doing here? I crossed my arms, holding my ribs with one hand and my opposite shoulder with the other.

"So, to help you with that, I'm going to lead you in an improvisation," Petra said. "Focus on sinking your weight into the floor."

I couldn't believe the critique was over. Ms. Kelly used to rant on and on until every single one of us felt like crap. Petra was actually offering a *solution*. Was this what they called *constructive* criticism? I unhooked my arms from my torso.

Petra smiled. "Let's start by lying down."

I lay on my back with my knees bent up, arms spread. My lower back released into the floor. My knees toppled to one side, my left leg swung across, and the momentum pulled me onto my stomach. I thought about what Lance had said: *express what's in your heart*. The sun slanted across the floor and I was hit with a memory of that afternoon with Kevin:

Before it happened, we looked into each other's eyes and he really saw me; I know he did. Separate colors made up the hazel of his eyes … green, amber, brown. But then, snap, his pupils dulled, and all signs that he knew me, let alone liked me, disappeared. He slid inside me, but I could have been anyone.

In the studio, I twisted and turned, flopping on the floor, a caricature of a restless sleeper. I didn't *want* to feel the weight of my limbs. I wanted to split off from my body, I wanted to forget. But after a few minutes of writhing, the movement took over. My arms and legs swept the floor. Soon I was sliding and popping into jackknifes, upside down, weight on my hands, following Petra's cues to move around the room. She guided us to a standing finish. I pretended to rise from a pile of tangled bed sheets. I kicked them to the side of the room.

"Good, good." Petra nodded and made eye contact with each of us in turn. "You've got *substance* now, you've got density. You want to bring all of that inner richness to the work."

Evening

Mom called tonight. "Hi, Nat."

Warmth filled my chest. "Hi, Mom." It's much easier to think fondly of someone when you're not living on top of each other. Besides, spending time with Sasha had made me feel lucky in the Mom department.

"You've had a couple of phone calls—one from Lisa."

I sucked in a breath. "What did she say?"

Was my luck going to hold? Could I really be both un-pregnant and uninfected?

"She said to tell you that she has good news. But the details can wait till you're back in town."

Perfect. I released my breath.

"I heard from Kevin, as well."

A bungee jump from a railroad trestle couldn't have made my stomach lurch more.

"Nat? Are you there?"

"Yeah." I tried to sound normal. "What did he say?"

He apologized to her for the party. He asked about me and about the yard and whether there was anything he could do. He gave her his number to pass on to me—the number where he's staying, that is. I'm pretty sure he's still transient.

Kevin must have charmed Mom, because she said if I wanted to call him, I could charge it to the calling card. "I really think he just wants to make amends."

Can she be that naïve? My impatience with her rushed back. A guy like Kevin never calls up just to apologize. He must want something. I wonder what Lisa would say? *Too little, too late,* I bet. *I really think you should forget him.*

Maybe Mom thinks if I'm dating, I'll be too distracted to care about *her* love life. Maybe she hopes that someone else will provide me with TLC (her pet acronym: Tender Loving Care), leaving her free to squander all her love on Marine. Poor Paige! I'll be all right, but a ten-year-old still needs a mother. I hope Mom pulls herself together before Paige gets back.

Still ... I *am* tempted to call Kevin. I wonder what he wants? And if he knows what happened to Sasha? It's calmer now that she has gone. That mean streak of hers is hardening into a permanent callus, and the things she said really stung. I worry about her, but I don't know how to help.

Saturday, August 21st

Petra's boyfriend Michel returned yesterday, so I packed up my things and moved to Monique's studio apartment. Besides a kitchenette, her room contains only a sofa (a.k.a. guest bed), a set of shelves, and a coffee table made from black plastic crates. She sleeps on a mattress in a walk-in closet and shares a bathroom with two neighbors down the hall.

This morning, before Monique left to get her hair cut, she said, "Let's go out dancing tonight."

"At a bar? I'm fifteen, remember?"

"Pfff. Fifteen going on twenty-one. Leave it to me, *chérie*."

Monique is still at the salon. The phone is sitting on the coffee table. This is probably the best chance I'm going to have to call Kevin. God, I want to! I can't believe we were living together like lovers for a week and then, boom—no contact at all. OK. Deep breath.

Afterwards ...

I didn't realize how mad I was.

Mad that he moved into my mother's house without an invitation, mad that I let him stay, mad that he spent my grocery money on beer and weed, mad that he had that party against my wishes, mad that his friends tore up the garden, and MAD that he seduced me! MAD! MAD!! Mad that I *let* him seduce me, too. But mad that he wouldn't realize that we needed to talk about it, that losing your virginity is a big deal, that it might upset me, and that above all we needed to use protection! All these feelings flooded me when he answered the phone. I really let him have it.

He listened, I'll give him that. He tried to soothe me. Just hearing his voice transported me to "our" lake, where arbutus leaves were turning color and water lapped the dock. The memory turned me on. I twisted on the couch and hugged a pillow to my stomach. I wanted to soften my voice and touch him with it, like a lover.

Instead, I described the embarrassing trip to the drugstore and the hideous appointment at the Sexual Health Clinic. "I'm *never* going through that again."

He was quiet for a minute. What was he thinking? What was he feeling?

"I'm sorry, Natalie," he said finally. "I guess I took advantage of you."

He exhaled heavily: he was smoking.

"But I wasn't calling just to apologize."

I *knew* it.

"You weren't?"

My heart was pounding. I wanted to hear in words what I'd seen in his eyes that afternoon. A confession of feeling.

"No." He paused and inhaled again. "I—I'd like to see you again."

That wasn't nearly enough. "I'm in Vancouver."

"Really?"

"Yeah, and I'm going out clubbing tonight."

"With who?"

I told Kevin what Monique had said: *When I'm finished with you, you won't even need fake ID.*

He snorted. "Watch out for older guys. They're only after one thing."

I sputtered. "*You're* an older guy, Kevin. What does that say about *you*?"

"There's an exception to every rule, Natalie."

"And you're it."

"That's right."

"Whatever."

When I hung up the phone, I was shaking.

Sunday, August 22nd

Last night I wore a backless halter top with Monique's leather pants and swept my hair into a French twist. Three-inch heels and dramatic makeup. Two of Monique's friends joined us: Nadia and Min. Nineteen-year-old Nadia and I look a little bit alike, and she lent me her driver's license. It passed inspection, and they let me in. Nadia joined us half an hour later, using her passport for ID.

It was dark, loud, and crowded. I needed a drink just to blunt my senses. The waitress didn't ask for ID. She just delivered what I ordered. I couldn't get over the freedom, the power. The others said I looked nineteen or twenty and fit in just fine. I could afford only two drinks and downed them one after another. Two coolers on a fairly empty stomach made me tipsy.

Black wavy hair, rippled arms, and a long body grabbed my attention—Kevin! The guy must have felt my eyes on his back. He turned around and caught me staring. Then grinned. Not Kevin at all, but cute. I grinned back and he approached and asked me to dance. I flung myself into the movement, at ease. The music changed and we stayed for a slow dance. He held me close, and the heat of his body aroused me. When the song ended, he led me to a velvety-cushioned seat. Across the bar, the trio of Monique, Nadia, and Min sipped their drinks and watched me over their straws. It felt good to know they were looking out for me. Hip hop music blasted and people grooved, like an MTV video, but live.

The guy, named Michael, bought me another vodka cooler. He talked about his car and the work he was doing on it. I really didn't care what he had to say—I was just hoping he would touch me again. Pretty soon he did. When I didn't respond to a question, he nudged me and then let his hand drape my thigh. I was hoping he would work his hand up my leg. But the waitress arrived with my drink and he lifted his hand off. He stretched his arm over the back of the seat and brushed his fingertips against my shoulder. I snuggled against him and turned up my face. He didn't have much choice but kiss me. It was soft and slow, the opposite of Kevin's.

He broke away. "I have to ask you how old you are."

I blurted, "Fifteen." I don't know why, except I was sick of secrets and lies.

He jumped back on the seat and retracted his arm. "Are you serious?"

"No, just kidding!"

But it was too late.

"I thought you were nineteen or twenty. What are you even *doing* in here? You could get yourself into a lot of trouble."

"What are you, the minor patrol?"

"My sister is eighteen and I wouldn't even want *her* in here. For God's sake, I'm twenty-four."

It was my turn to be surprised. "I thought *you* were nineteen or twenty. Anyway, I can take care of myself."

"That's not what it felt like to me. Man, I feel like I should turn you in."

"You wouldn't dare." I took a swig of the cooler.

He eyed the bottle and shook his head. "I bought liquor for a minor."

"That's right, you're an accessory, you can't turn me in."

He sighed. "You're right. I'll have to share it with you." He took the bottle from me and sipped. "Blech. How do you drink that sweet crap?"

"Easy." I snatched the bottle.

Michael turned his head away to think, then swiveled it back. "Okay." He slapped my thigh in a friendly way. "Here's the deal. I won't turn you in, but I'm going to keep my eye on you for the rest of the night."

"No more kissing?"

"Go dance with your friends, child."

I stuck out my tongue at him. I didn't appreciate being called a child. But he did watch out for me for the rest of the night. If any other guys started to move in on me, he would step in and join me, kind of like a bodyguard. We danced a few more times and chatted a bunch. I said things like, "You're *sure* you don't want another kiss?" just to tease him. It was so fun just to flirt. At the end of the night he said, "It was a pleasure to meet you. Do come back—in *four years!*"

I'm glad it turned out the way it did. Michael's reaction to my age has made me wonder, again, why Kevin would want to date someone so much younger. And my reaction to alcohol makes me think I should hold off in the future. I didn't get as drunk as the other girls, though, so I'm feeling pretty good today.

Night

When Monique stumbled out of her bedroom/closet at 10 a.m., she said—or croaked, actually—"I need some water!" Her French accent thickens in the morning. Once she had filled up a couple of water bottles, she said, "Best thing for a hangover is to sweat it out." We bought muffins and yogurt at the grocery store across the street, then bussed to Stanley Park and circled the sea wall on foot, a three-hour walk. Thickly-leaved trees bordered the path. Jagged, blue mountains loomed on the north shore. Crisp salt air rolled off the ocean and we breathed it in deep. Waves sloshed and slapped the wall. Every so often, a beach opened up and we would rest on a log for awhile. Nothing better than walking and talking. I learned a lot about Monique. For now, she waitresses to supplement her dance career, but she's going to train as a massage therapist: the human body fascinates her.

Tonight, we made Indian food—chicken curry and basmati rice with mango chutney—and drank mint tea. It's only nine. The sky hasn't yet faded to black, but sleep is dropping down, bringing sweet salt-air and blue wave dreams ...

Monday, August 23rd

I doubted myself during rehearsal again today. The others have all learned the piece, so I've lost the advantage I had last week. Lance and Petra have to reassure me constantly; otherwise, I feel myself shrinking.

After rehearsal, Petra took me aside and said it looked like I was holding back. She wanted me to dance bigger. I admitted that I was afraid of making mistakes and embarrassing myself in front of the professionals. "I thought so," she said. "You're starting to be 'careful.' If you're going to make a mistake, make it big!"

I couldn't imagine doing that. I stood there feeling miserable. When Petra hired me, she didn't realize how much propping up I was going to need.

"Remember when you couldn't look at me after the Dance-Is show?" She hugged me sideways, with one arm. "You thought I was going to be so mad at you for changing the counts."

I remembered that night all too clearly. "That's exactly the sort of screw-up I'm worried about."

"Natalie, don't you remember what I told you that night?"

I shook my head.

"You got it right. You danced from your emotional core, and that's what the audience saw. That's what's most important. I don't mean you should throw technique or choreography out the window, but what matters most is staying true to the mood of the piece."

It was becoming clear that Petra really meant what she was saying. This wasn't just about trying to make me feel better for messing up the counts.

"Why don't you come watch my tech rehearsal? It might be a good distraction for you."

In the empty theater, Petra performed a solo created by another choreographer for the same festival. At the beginning, she crouched and huddled, balled up like a seed pod in a dim cellar. Light stabbed like someone was opening a door, and a beam of bright sunshine flooded a narrow strip of stage. Petra started to unfurl towards the light, then the door slammed shut and she crumpled again. She repeated this sequence several times.

Finally, the door cracked open and the light stayed. Petra's arms unfolded and she grew to a standing position. She explored the narrow corridor of light as the music intensified into sustained, orchestral chords. Once she had established the boundaries of the space, Petra began to dance bigger, with jumps and turns, running from one end of the beam to the next, but always contained within the light, never stepping outside it. The music was fading and the door began to close. She twisted and turned in panic as she realized she was running out of lit space. I leaned forward, terrified that she would end up in the cellar again, wanting something to happen, some breakthrough.

Before the door could close on her, Petra escaped the beam of light. She began to zigzag in and out of it, making *it* a part of *her* pattern. She controlled the space. The door halted. Then it slowly widened, back to the previous width. Petra played a game. She circled the perimeter of the triangle of light, staying just outside it. The crack widened to include her. She did this twice more, each time pushing the light to expand. Then it became random. She danced anywhere on the stage, and the light swelled and shrank, no longer a cage for her but a playmate. At one point, the stage was flooded with light—a bright, shadowless noon time. At another it was pitch dark, then lit from the wings. I wondered how the piece would end. I hoped Petra wouldn't be returned to the box—and I got my wish. The last light effect made the stage look like a sun-dappled forest, and Petra ran and skipped in figure eights and circles, forwards and backwards, until finally she ran off the stage.

During the tech rehearsal, she had to break down the piece step by step so the lighting designer and the choreographer could make the cues. It would have been boring, but Petra took the opportunity to plumb each phrase for its deepest quality. Movements that would happen in a split second during the actual dance, she dwelled in sometimes for minutes. I was startled by how naked and vulnerable the gestures could be. I wanted to wrap her in my arms and hug her; I wanted to join hands and skip with her; I wanted to fight my way into the technicians' booth and learn how to shine the light she longed for and deserved.

By the time it was over, I'd been on a journey. Petra pulled me out of myself, and at the same time, I related to her. Now I see what bothered me about Ms. Kelly's choreography. It was purely physical. Her jazz moves isolated sexual energy, so the girls dancing weren't fully human, just eye candy. Petra's solo made me *feel*.

Tuesday, August 24th

The other night I asked Mom if she was going to bring Marine to Vancouver to see the show. Her breath sort of caught in her throat. "I'm sure she would love to come, but she doesn't like to impose on our family time."

I could hear how much it meant to her. "I don't mind. I like Marine. It would be nice if you brought her." It made my heart swell to say that.

"Thank you, Natalie. That's very generous. I'll invite her and let you know."

Tonight she confirmed that Marine is coming with her.

Too bad Paige won't be here. She will only miss the show by a couple of days.

Wednesday, August 25th

Lance seems to have a fountain inside. It fills him up with self-acceptance and spills over to his students. I soak up his instruction the way a plant absorbs water, and it makes me more expansive and daring.

The only problem is that, by the next day, the inspiration

leaks away and leaves me empty and wilted again. I could never teach. I can't even buoy myself up, let alone someone else.

Thursday, August 26th
DAD JUST CALLED!

That has to be the first unscheduled Dad-initiated phone call in YEARS. Okay, it was obviously Mom-initiated, since how else did he get Monique's phone number? (I've dropped a few hints about cell phones making it easier to get hold of people, especially nomadic performers like me, but so far no dice. Not surprising, since Mom loathes technology. On the other hand, Dad lives and breathes it—can't he get Paige and me on some family plan? Or would that depend on *living in the same province*? Oh, no. I was in a good mood. Here I go again ...)

Dad put Vi and Paige on the phone, and everyone wished me good luck and said they would have loved to see the show. Bittersweet. Why can't Dad live out here, anyway? Plenty of other kids' parents have stayed close by after a divorce. They make a commitment not to move until the kids are eighteen. That's what becoming a parent is: a commitment. Dad never seemed to grasp that fact. It interfered with his *bliss*. (Gag.) At least he showed some responsibility and got a vasectomy. Otherwise, he probably would have done the same thing all over again with Vi, who doesn't have kids. I wonder if she's disappointed. She met Dad at thirty-five, just when her biological alarm clock should have been going off. I have a feeling he didn't tell her about the vasectomy until after she had fallen for him. I don't think it shows too much, the scars I mean, or, actually, I don't know about that. I've never asked—eww!

Thankfully, Monique just came home and distracted me. She made me sniff her clothes: "Do I smell like fish grease?" She went out for a drink with a guy after work and worried about her odor the whole time. "I hate working in a restaurant. My hair stinks as well."

"When you're a massage therapist, you will only smell of essential oils."

"*Mais oui.*" She lit patchouli incense and headed for the shower, calling out that we should go to the Blue Zone for a cast party on Saturday night.

I hope we just go out for food instead. I can't face the whole lying-about-my-age thing again right away.

Friday, August 27th

Over the past two weeks, I've gathered from dressing room conversations that Beth is out of work, Katrina is breaking up with her boyfriend, and Halle's father is dying of prostate cancer. Monique, of course, is working full-time and trying to save money for massage school. But everyone puts their stresses aside when they enter the studio, and magic happens. Fatigue melts away when we start to move.

After our final run-through today, Petra pulled me aside and said she was delighted with my work. She said I'm showing an emotional maturity that is surprising in someone my age, and that she can't tell anymore that I'm younger than the other dancers in the piece.

I owe it all to her and Lance. Not sure what will happen on Saturday without class or rehearsal before the show.

Saturday, August 28th

Wow. Can't believe they all showed up!

To start at the beginning: arriving backstage alone was nerve-wracking. The dancers from the other choreographers' pieces huddled in clusters and either ignored me, or looked me up and down like I was in the wrong place. A woman whose silver makeup made her look like the Tin Man in the *Wizard of Oz* was hairspraying her bangs. With one eye shut and a hand shielding her open eye, she said, "Who're you looking for?"

"Petra Moss?" I couldn't keep the question mark out of my voice.

"Other dressing room." Spritz. Spritz.

I coughed. "Thank you."

Next door, I found Petra, Monique, and the others. "There you are!" Petra said. She hugged me. "Do you need any help getting ready?"

She pinned me into my costume and touched up my hair. The close quarters made it hard to warm up, but I followed the others in Pilates exercises on the floor.

We were third up in the first half. When our five-minute call came, we held hands in a circle. We breathed together to center ourselves, then entered the wings one by one and picked our way among shin-high light fixtures and electrical cords. Crew members dressed in black were standing by to handle props and set changes. We slid into place behind heavy velvet curtains. I glimpsed the audience. Although it was dark, light reflected off people's faces, especially their glasses. Adrenaline surged through my body and my muscles twitched. Too late, Beth pulled me back, and I remembered the simple rule: If you can see them, they can see you. I was acting like a kid again.

As the lights came up, we *sensed* each other to know the timing. Eye contact and synchronized breath joined us into a larger organism. We gave weight and received it; we lifted each other. As the music sped up and grew louder, dissonant notes made us jump higher, push harder, and split from each other. As we spoked in our own directions, I felt the thrill of near-collision. These women commanded the space, and it took all I had to match their power.

I made it into the wings, where I had a few bars to catch my breath. As my lungs heaved, it hit me: *I am performing professionally.* I nearly missed my cue and Katrina pushed me between the shoulder blades. She and I were supposed to cross together, as rivals, and it took me a couple of counts to catch up.

I pressed on for the rest of the piece, but it felt more like a dress rehearsal. The music, the lighting, the stage, and the movement didn't really coalesce anymore. At least it rang true when I stumbled, confused and alone, across the stage. I was surrounded by darkness, stripped of support, forced to rely on myself. Anyone who did cross my path was likely an enemy who couldn't be trusted. Safety came only from solitude. But solitude brought pain. I filled that solo with so much emotion that I almost lost control.

Afterwards, Petra ran backstage right away. She handed each of us a long-stemmed red rose and kissed us on the cheek. "You were wonderful. So fully invested in the movement." Her kindness made me all the more determined to do a better job the next night.

By the time I'd changed out of my costume and washed off the makeup, the show was practically over. I waited in the lobby.

When the ushers propped open the doors, I spotted Mom and Marine inside the theater and was watching them slowly progress up the aisle when a voice called, "Natalie!" I spun around, not quite believing what I heard. Streaking across the lobby from the far aisle was Paige. With sun-bleached hair, a freckled face, a new white dress, and sandals. She looked older, but maybe it was just the clothes. She flung herself around my neck, and I spun her like we were on the front lawn in our bathing suits, playing in the sprinkler. "Paige! What are you *doing* here?"

"Dad and Vi brought me out to see you."

"Dad?"

A long cardboard box appeared under my nose, and when I looked up, I saw my father. He had aged. He had more gray hairs, and his face sagged a bit, like he was tired. He was wearing a brightly patterned, short-sleeved shirt, tan khakis, and docksiders. He could have fit into a catalog for a company like L. L.Bean or J. Crew—except for the shirt, which had a little too much personality.

I analyzed his appearance to avoid hugging him, I guess. I was too shocked to move. Bringing up the rear was his girlfriend, Vi. Her highlighted hair was pulled back in a low ponytail and held with a clip. She wore pink pedal pushers, a sleeveless white blouse, and sandals with delicate straps. Her toes sloped down at a steep angle—she would definitely have a hard time with pointe work—and her toenails were painted silvery mauve.

"Hi, Natalie," Vi said. "That was fantastic."

"What are you guys doing here?"

Vi resettled her purse. (It had short straps and sat more or less in her armpit, which looked uncomfortable.) I expected to hear about a business meeting or the wedding of one of Vi's friends, but apparently they came out on purpose to see me. Dad found a pair of tickets on eBay and changed Paige's return date.

Vi nodded at the box. "Aren't you going to open it?"

A dozen pink roses lay in a bed of baby's breath.

"Thank you. This is—such a surprise."

It was all I could muster. I hugged Dad and then Vi, silent tears welling up. Dad felt almost as alien to me as his girlfriend did.

He said, "Should we have warned you we were coming?"

I shook my head, then ducked to smell the bouquet. I slung my arm around Paige's shoulders. "Did you help to pick these out?"

She nodded. "I knew pink roses were your favorite." She reached into the box and pulled the flowers to her nose, then looked past me. "Mom!"

Mom's sandalwood scent reached me just before she did. She hugged me with Paige clinging to her other side. "Well done, Natalie! Hello, Paige, you monkey!" Mom wore a long skirt and flat, wide sandals with thick straps. Her hair was loose and a little fuzzy, the gray hairs undisguised.

Marine offered her hand to shake. "A beautiful performance, Natalie. Such tremendous emotional depth." She was wearing a handmade, multicolored shirt and a funky pair of jeans. Her square shoulders made her look confident.

Dad said, "Hello, Denise. You remember Vi."

Mom said, "Of course. Hello, Vi."

Dad and Vi looked at Marine expectantly. Mom didn't pick up on the cue—she must have been extra nervous—so I jumped in. "Dad, Vi, this is Marine," I said. They shook hands, and in the mix, Mom shook hands with Dad and Vi, too. Mom and

Vi had met before, but only once, and Mom and Dad—well, maybe they were renewing their acquaintance, or else reconciling their differences. It felt like an impromptu ceremony. The sort of broken-family reunion that normally only happens at weddings.

Things warmed up when Marine complimented Dad on his shirt. He mentioned a tailor he has discovered in Mississauga, and Marine egged him on with questions that only someone who sews would know to ask. It was kind of cute. I wondered whether Dad and Vi grasped the *nature* of Mom and Marine's relationship. Was it obvious just from her presence? Whenever Mom took a breath or cleared her throat to speak after a pause in the conversation, I half-hoped and half-dreaded that she was going to make a "coming out" announcement. It hasn't happened yet.

Saturday, August 28th—night
We peaked the second night. Synergy: we held each other's gaze, tightened our timing, upped the intensity. "You electrified the audience!" Petra said to us afterwards.

I sailed into the lobby on endorphins. My family must have noticed how much better I'd performed. I imagined Kevin's eyes on me, too. He might have heard about the show from Sasha and come to surprise me. Anything could happen.

I stationed myself next to the concession. Dance enthusiasts streamed past, but no one greeted me. Not Mom or Marine, not Paige, not Dad or Vi, and, most definitely, not Kevin. My legs trembled and my upper lip broke out in sweat. I'd barely eaten before the show and my blood sugar was plummeting.

I found a payphone near the bathrooms and called Mom's hotel. She was shocked to hear I was alone.

"Aren't Paige and your dad there?"

"No." I bent back my knee and let my foot swing so that my toe stubbed the wall. *Thwunk*. Pull back. *Thwunk*.

"I spoke to her earlier and she said they were going. Marine and I decided to let the Ontario folks have you to themselves. They must have had the same idea."

Translation: no one wanted to repeat the encounter from the night before. Let me guess who's to blame: *Vi* probably felt exposed as an airhead in the face of artists and teachers. Either that or she looked down on the West Coast hippies. And *Marine* probably felt uncomfortable since Mom hasn't had the guts to come out and introduce her as her girlfriend. I bet she has been out as a lesbian for years and doesn't want to go back into the closet. Or, maybe those two wanted to have a final night of "love" before Mom resumes full-time motherhood.

It didn't matter why: I was alone. Again.

I hung up and wandered back into the lobby, tracking the pattern of triangles inside circles on the carpet. I kept my eyes on the floor to hide my tears.

"Natalie?"

A male voice startled me. I brushed the back of my hand across my eyelids before raising my head. Kind blue eyes met mine: Lance Irving. "That was a beautiful performance. Your movement has matured so much in the past month. You must have gone through a growth spurt."

I gulped and nodded.

"Are you all right?"

Normally, I would have answered, "I'm fine." But I couldn't lie to Lance. He was too sincere. "My family are all in town, but none of them bothered to come a second time. They're obviously not interested in my dancing, or they would have come back."

I expected him to disagree, but he surprised me.

"Sometimes the people we're related to by birth, we don't have much in common with. They care about us, and we care about them, but we don't always understand each other. Fortunately, as we get older, we find other supporters and role models who share our passion, and who can understand and appreciate what we do."

He clasped his hands behind his back and turned his head away from me. I could tell he was debating whether to add something because I do that too. Usually, the person I'm talking to turns to see what I'm looking at, but I'm only gathering my thoughts. When Lance faced me again, he gave me a look that said: *Are you ready for this?* I nodded, and he carried on.

"My family disapproved of my dancing because I was a boy and it wasn't manly. I come from a long line of auto mechanics. They expected me to carry on the family business, never mind that I couldn't tell a wrench from a screwdriver. That was hard enough, but when I came out as gay, my family disowned me altogether. I had to find a new family in the dance community. And that worked," he said with a smile, "up until—" He lowered his head and cut himself off. I bet he was thinking of AIDS. Last year, at the benefit concert for people living with HIV, one of the emcees said the virus had taken a great toll on the dance community. "It won't be that hard for you, Natalie. You'll always have your family—you're lucky they were all here last night. But from now on, there will also be people like Petra, and myself, who validate you in a different way—as a fellow artist."

Something burst open under my sternum when he said that. I laughed a little bit, but tears spilled out too.

My lonely journey across the stage in Petra's dance summed up my *life*. Shutting myself into my room during the long months it took my parents to divorce. Yelling, "Go away! Leave me alone!" anytime someone knocked at the door. Once, it was Paige, and I felt so terrible for shouting at her that I grabbed my most trusted companion—a penguin with enormous, floppy wings and patient eyes—and darted after her. "You can carry Penny." I thrust the stuffed toy at her. The two almost matched in size, and Paige had to waddle like a penguin herself as she carried Penny down the hall.

All this time, I've longed for my parents to *see* me, *love* me, *get* me. What they offer is never enough, even now: Sure, Dad flew all the way to Vancouver, but he ditched me the second night. He breaks my heart over and over. I'm continually let down.

Lance's words didn't make the sadness disappear. But for a second, I saw my life through a wider lens. I don't need my family quite so much if I have other ways to belong.

I'd been staring into space, and Lance was watching with concern. I took a breath and tried to compress the tangle of emotions into words. All that came out was, "Thank you."

He hugged me, and squashed up against him, I wondered, what made him so warm? How could he have enough caring inside him to spare for me, just one of his many students, and a new one at that?

He released me from the embrace as Petra and Monique walked up. "We're going to Havana for tapas—want to come?" Petra said. "It's on me."

"Sure." I wiped away the last of my tears.

It was warm enough to sit outside and, luckily, a table opened up on the restaurant's terrace as we arrived. The clink of cutlery offset the revving of car engines. Hip people strolled past on Commercial Drive. We joined the Saturday night din and toasted our successful show. I ordered a tomato and bocconcini salad, and we shared yam fries and tiger prawns.

Petra said, "Lance, did you tell Natalie the news?"

I looked up. Lance had just bitten into a prawn. We all waited for him to chew and swallow. "I'm teaching in Victoria at Eastside Dance, starting the third week of September."

"You're kidding!" I'd forgotten he was considering a move. Training with Lance would change everything. "For how long?"

He dabbed his mouth with a napkin. "I'm trying it out for the fall."

Petra winked at me. "You'll have to convince him to stay."

I sat back and took it all in. Monique's French accent, Petra's bell-like voice, and Lance's bass tones made a fugue against the background roar. The evening air was cooling, and hairs bristled on my arms. A vertical line plumbed my center. As the others discussed their next projects, I dreamed up a plan for the following day.

Sunday, August 29th

Dad, Paige, and Vi were suiting up by the rental kiosk when Mom, Marine, and I found them. Under helmets, wrist guards, knee and elbow pads, I barely recognized them—especially Dad. Never much of an athlete, he rarely wore shorts, let alone protective gear. But when I'd proposed a picnic in Stanley Park, he'd said, "Great! We can rollerblade beforehand." Who knew Vi had inspired him to start blading? I obviously needed to ask more questions during our phone calls.

"You look like you're ready to take on the Oilers!" I said.

He coughed. "I don't know about that." But he stood at ease on his blades, pushing fingerless gloves down to the webbing.

Paige swiveled 360 degrees. "I've already lost my balance once, and it didn't hurt at all. You're going to try, aren't you?"

"How can I resist?"

Mom and Marine had no trouble resisting. They struck out to claim a picnic spot while I wrestled with equipment. The kiosk faced the park, and we had to cross a busy street to reach it. The other three shot across the intersection as soon as the light changed. I wished I'd carried my blades: I was *not* ready for traffic, even the pedestrian kind. I stepped off the curb and lurched into a man in an electric wheelchair that sported a Canadian flag. I grabbed the back of his chair to steady myself. "Sorry! Excuse me! I don't know how to rollerblade!"

"Hang on for your life! I'll give you a ride."

I held my legs stiff and my feet together. The bumpy road sent vibrations up my spine and jostled me to the marrow. Had the manufacturers forgotten the shock absorbers on these things? People in cars idling at the light had a front-row seat to our performance. One couple pointed and laughed. I averted my eyes from the rest. Once we reached safety, I shook the man's hand and thanked him.

"Anytime!" He laughed. "Folks on wheels need to stick together. You be careful now."

A gentle slope led down to the blading path. I took one look at it and headed for the grass. I clumped sideways down the hill, like I was on skis. They were waiting for me at the bottom. Dad and Vi gave me an all-too-quick overview of the basics, and then led the way. I was amazed at Dad's poise. Paige kept pace. They'd obviously done a lot of this in Ontario. Trailing behind, I learned by watching to bend my knees, tip forward at the waist, drop my weight, and swing my arms. Stanley Park sped past in a blue green blur. Every so often we had to screech to a halt when the trail bent or converged or we hit a patch of congestion. When we stopped, Vi gasped, "Those mountains! That water!" We bladed around the perimeter of the park in a fraction of the time it had taken Monique and I to walk it.

Mom and Marine were waiting on a grassy slope close to Second Beach. When we zoomed up, they were unpacking bagels, cream cheese, nectarines, and grapes.

"I'm starved!" Paige said.

"Me too!" Dad and Vi chimed in unison.

"Me three," I said.

"Me Tarzan!" Marine pounded her chest.

"No, you Jane!" Mom said.

Paige smacked her lips. "Let's eat."

We divvied up the fruit. Mom said, "Is anyone going to vie with me for the last nectarine?"

Vi said, "I'll *vie* with you!" She convulsed with laughter, as if realizing for the first time that her name had a double meaning. She'd missed out on years of silliness, and she laughed long and hard to make up for it. It was contagious: Soon Dad, Paige, and I were clutching our ribs. Rollerblading had made us downright giddy.

Mom said, with mock exasperation, "You four!"

Marine opened her mouth to respond to Mom, and we realized that she, too, had been laughing, but silently, until then. "Eugh," she sputtered. She laughed even harder.

"Wha-ha-hat?" It sounded like Mom was inhaling laughing gas. She pressed Marine's knee.

Marine said, "*Eu-phor-ia!*"

Our bellies shook until they were sore.

"Do you feel outnumbered by all these hysterical women, Will?"

I stared at Mom. She never called Dad by his name. It was always, "your father" or "he."

Dad was leaning back, hands planted on the grass. Ruddy cheeks made him look healthy. "I don't know." He sunk his weight into his arms so that his shoulders nearly touched his ears and his chin sunk to his chest. "I sort of feel like one of the girls!"

We dug into the food. Mom sliced the last nectarine in two and passed half of it to Vi. A large bottle of water made the rounds. We'd forgotten drinking glasses and didn't want to trade spit, so we threw back our heads, tipped the bottle upside down, and held it inches above our gaping mouths. Water gushed into throats but also down necks and shirts. We shrieked and giggled some more.

A bit of cream cheese dotted the middle of Marine's cheek. When I caught her eye, I touched the same spot on my own face. She winked and dabbed herself with a napkin. She seemed to fit in with us. Had her family disowned her, like Lance's? Some day, I would ask.

"Thanks for bringing the food, Mom. You too, Marine." The picnic more than made up for being stranded at the theater the night before.

"Yes!" Vi said. She had just bit into her half of the nectarine and had to slurp to catch the juice. "Thanks, you two. It's delicious."

Monday, August 30th

Monique suggested that we make sushi and stay up late in honor of my departure. "It's going to be lonely without you," she said.

"It's not so easy making friends in a new city. I've enjoyed your company."

"Me too," I said. "You've been a great hostess. But, we don't live far apart. You should come and visit me in Victoria next!"

While we were rolling the sushi, Petra called to say she had found a black backpack in her apartment. I was about to say it wasn't mine when it hit me: Sasha had left her bag at Petra's, and I'd agreed to take it back to Victoria. Petra offered to bring it to Monique's. Ten minutes later, the bag containing the stolen, peacock-green-and-blue dress had joined my innocent luggage by the door of Monique's apartment.

Worrying about the dress made me short with Monique. She asked if I was dreading going home. I finally confessed my dilemma, and we considered our options:

1) Return the dress to the store.

My conscience liked this option best. The dress hadn't been paid for, and it belonged back in the store. But we would physically have to visit the store—one of those high-end Robson Street outlets with the snobby, picture-perfect clerks who make you feel like you just crawled out of a hovel and are infested with body lice even as they flash you a bleached-teeth grin. Worse, I would have to say, "Uh, my friend, uh, took this dress and now I'm returning it." They would be like, "Oh, your *friend* took it, did she? Excuse me while I call security so they can talk to your *friend*." Plus, they probably wouldn't take it back; they would make me pay for it. And I don't want to and can't afford it.

2) Slip into the store with the dress in a shopping bag, set it down, and skedaddle.
This seemed like a reasonable alternative, but abandoned packages scare people so much these days that the staff would call the bomb squad, the store would be evacuated, and we would be charged with impersonating terrorists. We crossed off Option 2.

3) Just return the bag to Sasha, no comment.
Pro: I wouldn't atone for Sasha's crime, which really wasn't my responsibility anyway.
Con: I would become an *accessory* by transporting stolen goods.

4) Tell my mom and let her deal with it.
With her adult authority, she could probably get away with returning the dress and saying she suspected her teenaged daughter's disturbed friend had stolen it. The downside: Sasha would get in trouble since Mom would feel obliged to tell Sasha's parents. And what if the store forced her to pay for the dress?

We were stumped. Monique said the easiest thing to do was take the bag to Sasha and just forget about the dress. But every time I thought about delivering the stolen goods, anger flared inside my ribcage, like heartburn. I didn't want to be implicated in what she'd done.

Finally, Monique came up with the idea of depositing the dress in a Salvation Army donation box. Relief washed through me and my mind cleared. Monique knew where to find a box and, though it was 11 p.m., wanted to do it right away. A wind had picked up and the streets were nearly abandoned. Rustling startled me: a rat, or bits of wrapper, or dried leaves, scuttled across the road. A gate slammed shut. Monique said, "Isn't this exciting? I love an adventure." I huddled into my hoodie and buried my fists in the pockets.

A streetlight towered over the padlocked deposit box. I pulled out the dress and we both gasped at its beauty: now a midnight blue that blended into the night and poured like silky water over my hands. I had definite doubts about whether we were doing the right thing. But Monique said all the donations went to a good cause. So I folded up the dress, replaced it in its paper bag, and gently pushed it into the drop box. It was a bit like mailing a letter: Once the bag slid through the narrow opening in the metal container—the size of a garbage dumpster—it was final. No changing our minds.

The burden was lifted without involving any adults—well, in fact, Monique is an adult, but the more time I spent with her, the more it seemed like twenty-two is just fifteen plus freedom. She said she didn't feel the age gap either.

Tuesday, August 31st

Mom sat, I sprawled, and Paige darted around us on the outside deck of the ferry. We didn't talk much, just watched the islands and basked in the sun. Paige called out when she spotted a seal. I loved being homeward bound in our familiar trio.

Earlier, over a farewell breakfast, Dad teased me about staying out of trouble. "I don't want to be getting any more phone calls from the Victoria police!" I blushed—I'd practically forgotten about that. I suppose that's one reason he made the trip out at the last minute. People accuse delinquent kids of "seeking atten-tion." Well, apparently it works. Was Sasha so lucky, I wonder? I have to call her soon.

Wednesday, September 1st

Got hold of Sasha on her cell. She's just moved into an apart-ment with her dad. We're meeting up tomorrow so I can give her the backpack. We can't hang out long because tomorrow Mom's taking Paige and me back-to-school shopping.

Thursday, September 2nd

Sasha and I picked a park midway between my house and her new place as our meeting spot. When I arrived on my bike, the park was deserted except for a little girl twisting on the kiddie swing set. She was hanging her head so that her long, straight hair fell in a curtain over her face. Her hair shifted and swayed as she moved on the swing. I was wondering where her guardian was—little kids are never allowed out by themselves like that, at least not around here—when she flipped up her head and looked straight at me. It was Sasha, her legs bent up underneath her. It jolted me, as if she had just snuck up behind me and said, "Boo!" I managed to wave. I pedaled across the bumpy field, set the pack on the grass, and crammed my body into the neighboring swing.

She didn't look at me or the pack. I asked her how she liked her dad's new place and she shrugged. I fingered the swing's chains and waited for her to speak. She sat there in silence.

Finally, I gave her an opening. "You know the dress?" I nudged the bag. She winced. "Monique and I, uh ..."

When I hesitated, Sasha jerked her head in alarm. "You *what?*"

"We, uh … got rid of it." It sounded like we'd dumped a body in the river. I laughed nervously.

Her face relaxed for a second, then she frowned and hung her head. "Good." She pushed the swing back as far as she could, kicked up her legs, and yanked on the chains. Her back tipped so that she faced the sky. On the return pass, she tucked her legs out of the way and just cleared the ground. She pumped hard till she reached maximum height. The whole set vibrated. But the swing hung so low that the instant she loosened the tuck, her knees scraped the ground. "Oww!" She howled and projected her legs, rocking back and forth in an L-shape until the momentum died down. "Fucking kiddie swing." She inspected her knees. Dirty abrasions welled with blood.

"You should clean those up."

She eyed her scrapes: raw red patches and tiny curls of white skin, smudged with dirt.

"Don't they sting?"

She shrugged again. "So what?"

More silence.

Finally, I spilled. "I saw you running down the street that day with a pair of jeans flapping behind you. Then later we heard that your dad came and got you. You got caught, didn't you?"

"So?"

I wasn't expecting that. It took me a second to come up with something else to say. "So … I bet your dad was pissed off."

She tsked. "He treats me like a fucking criminal!" She spat on the ground and rifled in the pocket of her windbreaker. She pulled out a package of cigarettes and a clear plastic lighter.

I couldn't hold back. "I guess bad habits run in families, huh?"

She flicked the lighter and scowled at me over the flame. "What's it to you?"

I shook my head and waved the smoke away.

She inhaled and exhaled a couple of times. "You really saw me that day?" She sounded kind of proud.

"Yeah. What happened after that?"

The corners of her mouth twitched, and she took another drag. "The store called the cops, and the cops are just crawling through that neighborhood, right? I was running and that caught their attention. If I'd been smarter I would have, like, changed my appearance right away—pulled my hair down out of the ponytail, taken my jacket off, put my sunglasses on—anything so that I didn't match the description they sent out. But at the time all I thought about was running. When I saw the first cop car, I just panicked. I dropped the jeans and took off. If I'd known the neighborhood better, I would have made it for sure. But they must have called another cruiser. I was just coming around a corner when a cop stepped out. He blocked my way and grabbed me in, like, a big bear hug, but he wasn't hugging me, he was busting me. It was all downhill from there." Sasha had perked up during the story, but now she slumped in the swing again. "I gave them a fake name at first—Daisy Miller popped into my head for some reason—but they somehow knew it was fake."

"That's the title of a book. My mom has it. Didn't you get roped into watching the video with us one night?"

Sasha smirked. "Yeah, probably. That figures. I totally should have had my alias ready. They convinced me they would find out my real name sooner or later and that it would all go much better for me if I just told them. So I did, and then of course they called Dad. Pigs! They took me back to the park to get the jeans and then back to the store. They made me apologize to those bitchy clerks! I could have slapped them. All of them!" She lifted one leg and slammed her heel into the dirt over and over. Chunks of dry, pale earth scattered and flew. An underlying strip emerged, dark and moist. Ash built up on the end of her cigarette; she seemed to forget to smoke.

"Do you have to go to court, or what?"

She expelled her breath. "No, the store supposedly has a policy where they don't press charges if it's a first-time offense and you're under eighteen. But they make you pay for the shit even if you don't want it. I left the jeans there. They were in perfectly good condition, and there's no way I was going to pay for them. But they made Dad give them his credit card number and now I have to pay him back. It's so fucked up."

I couldn't quite believe what I was hearing. I don't know if Sasha has changed a lot in the past few months, or if I never really knew her as well as I thought.

Pretty soon after that I had to leave. To go *clothes shopping*, how ironic. All afternoon, I noticed *Shoplifters Will be Prosecuted* signs, surveillance cameras, security tags, posters with mug shots. All the people in the "wanted" posters were men. Anytime a girl's photo was taped to a lamppost or a window or stuck on a bulletin board, the heading read: *Missing*.

I suppose I should be glad Sasha's a shoplifter, not a runaway: better to be "Wanted" than "Missing." After all, she was *trying* to run away when I found her on the ferry that day. Maybe I saved her once. But now what?

Tuesday, September 7th—first day of school

Sasha showed up at school during morning assembly. From our old spot in the bleachers, I saw her slip into the auditorium and take a seat on the floor. She wore a black T-shirt, black jeans, and a choker. During the announcements, she bent forward and picked at her nail polish.

The new principal—a middle-aged transplant from Langford—introduced herself with a pep talk. Otherwise, the assembly echoed a million assemblies past, right down to the way they called out students' names in closing. But unlike the award winners in June, these students had to report to the office. I tensed when I heard *Sasha Varkosky* and found her again in the crowd. She must have been searching for me, too, because our eyes met.

I mouthed, "Wait," and pointed to myself, then to her.

I jostled my way to where she was leaning against the auditorium wall, her arms crossed. "I'm not going to the fucking office."

"Nice to see you too."

She simpered.

"Come on, I'll go with you. They'll find you sooner or later."

Ms. Pucker-Face from the June ceremony, still second-in-command in the principal's office, was sorting students into lines. Her reading glasses hung around her neck. "Hello, Natalie," she said. The power of her memory was truly alarming. "Shouldn't you be in class?"

"I'm here with my friend, Sasha."

"I would think Sasha is quite old enough to look after herself."

Sasha sucked air through her teeth. "Actually, Nat is the only thing standing between you and a black eye," she muttered.

"Take it easy." I touched her elbow. "I'm not going anywhere."

Ms. Pucker-Face herded us into the line for students whose registrations showed some "irregularity." We waited our turn. Some kids bit their nails; others stared at the floor. Sasha crossed her arms and tapped her foot.

When we finally reached the desk, the office secretary, a soft-spoken young man, typed in Sasha's name. "The records show that you phoned in an address change last week."

"So?"

I raised my eyebrows at Sasha. Sure, she was living with her dad, but it wasn't like her to volunteer personal information to the authorities. Besides, their arrangement could change.

She registered my surprise. "What? I want her *out* of my life."

At Sasha's tone of voice, Ms. P-F drifted over. She hovered beside the young man, raised her eyeglasses, and read the computer screen. "Is there a problem?"

I tried to help. "Sasha's family has two households."

Ms. P-F spouted the rules: Sasha was entitled to attend Oakridge *only* if she was living *at least* part-time with a parent or guardian in the school district. Nobody from outside the catchment area could be accommodated this year.

"Should we call the parent in the school district?" Judging by the mildness of the secretary's voice, he meant well.

"No!" Sasha shouted.

"Excellent idea," Ms. P-F said. She must have heard Sasha threatening to give her a black eye. She fixed a vengeful gaze on her and dialed, putting the call on speaker phone. I glanced around at the other students still waiting to have their registration problems sorted out.

"Could we please have some privacy?" I said.

No one paid me any attention.

Sasha's mom picked up on the third ring.

"Mrs. Varkosky, this is Ms. Butterwell from the principal's office at Oakridge High."

"What do you want?"

Ms. Pucker-Face/Butterwell half-laughed, half-coughed. *Like mother, like daughter*, she must have thought. "Mrs. Varkosky, we're trying to determine the residence of your daughter, Sasha."

It was Mrs. V's turn to snort. "I haven't laid eyes on her in two weeks. Why? Is she in trouble again?"

"Not exactly." The principal's assistant bared her teeth at Sasha.

"I can't believe you're doing this," Sasha said.

"Sasha? Is that you?" Mrs. V.'s voice trembled up from the speaker.

"For God's sake, stop this!" I gestured behind me to the waiting students. Some of them were enjoying the diversion; others looked worried that theirs might be the next family drama to be broadcast. "This is a private matter."

Ms. Butterwell spoke again. "Mrs. Varkosky, we just need to know. Will Sasha be living at your residence during the coming school year?"

"You'd better ask *her* that. I've told her she's welcome—"

"Welcome? Welcome to be ragged on nightly by a drunk?"

"Sasha." I whispered and squeezed her arm. "Not here."

"—but she informs me she's living full-time with her father."

"Thank you, Mrs. Varkosky. That's all we need to know." Ms. Butterwell terminated the call before Mrs. V. could reply and turned to Sasha. "I'm referring you to Victoria High."

"You can't do this!"

"I have to do this. This school is full. Now if you'll excuse me, there's a line of students waiting behind you."

Sasha scowled and flushed red. I offered to walk home with her.

"No. I'll get a ride."

She took off before I could say anything more. I checked my timetable and then the hall clock. First period was almost over, so I used the washroom and then snuck outside to wait for the buzzer. In the pick-up and drop-off zone across the field, Sasha approached a car I didn't recognize, yanked open the passenger door, and got in. The mystery car pulled out and sped away.

Wednesday, September 8th

The PE teacher took us outside for the first class. Somehow, it felt cruel. The sunshine made it that much harder to accept being imprisoned in school. Hobbled horses must feel like this: surrounded by green pastures but unable to run free.

Last spring, Sasha and I planned our schedules together. In almost every class this week, I've had to listen to the teacher call her name. The first time, I turned my head to the right where Sasha used to sit. The teacher called her name a second time, louder. When I said, "Sasha doesn't go here anymore," the pit of my stomach ached. But as much as I miss her, I don't know if I can hang out with her anymore. She's so angry, and I'm worried she'll keep getting into trouble. My stomach aches worse to think of it.

A pair of hands clamped over my eyes from behind.

"Sasha?"

"No. Guess again." The voice was disguised in a falsetto.

"I give up."

The hands released me and I spun around. "Claire!"

She seemed even taller than usual—she must have shot up another inch over the past couple of months. Her long, lean arms and legs looked ready for anything. She played volleyball at the beach all summer, when she wasn't scooping ice cream. And it shows: she's still tanned and her hair has bleached blonde in the sun.

"Want to be partners?"

"Huh?"

Claire laughed. "Didn't you hear anything the teacher just said?"

All around us, kids were turning to each other and talking. The teacher was hauling out grass hockey equipment and soccer balls. "What's going on?"

Claire explained that the PE teachers are trying something new. They want students with training in various sports to lead an introductory class session in it. It's especially encouraged if you have a friend from your team or club in your PE class, so you can co-teach. Kids who don't teach a class have to write an essay on a physical activity that interests them.

"Are you going to teach volleyball?" I said.

"I just asked. The teacher would rather I didn't, because everyone already learned it in Grade Nine." Claire cracked a smile. "That's where you come in."

"Oh, no!"

"Oh, yes! Let's co-teach a dance class."

Someone came up behind Claire. "What's up, defects?"

Claire whirled around. "I beg your pardon? Oh. Jamie. Hi."

Jamie held her hips, elbows wide. "Defects, as in, you *defected* from Dance-Is. Rhymes with rejects."

Claire and I spun to face each other. "You quit?" we said at the same time.

"You first," I said.

"I'm trying out for the volleyball team," she said. "I can always go back to dance later. But *you*—you love dance!"

"I know. I'm going to Eastside this year for modern."

"Like I said," Jamie drawled, "rhymes with rejects."

"You should team up with Claire to teach dance," I said to Jamie.

Claire's mouth dropped open and her eyes flashed at me.

Jamie held up both palms and nodded with false modesty. "Thanks, but I'm taken. I'm doing weight lifting with Nick. The teacher's all over our coed approach. You know, Nick's a guy—"

"—and you're a girl." Claire nodded and smiled with relief.

"But, hey," Jamie pointed back and forth from me to Claire, "you two should teach dance."

Claire spread her arms and looked at me. "See? That's what I think."

"Because I could probably get out of that class," Jamie continued. "I mean, how boring would that be for *me*?"

Claire narrowed her eyes. "Thanks for the vote of confidence, Jamie."

The idea of teaching makes me too tense to move. I can't exactly teach dance when I'm paralyzed, can I? Writing a paper would be a thousand times easier. Claire must be out of her mind.

Thursday, September 9th

A small, beat-up brown car like the one Sasha drove off in the other day was parked at the curb when school got out. A throng of kids was heading down the path to the road, so I snuck in behind them. I had to cross the street to stay hidden, but I glimpsed the driver's curly black hair and muscled shoulder. Kevin, I think.

My heart pounded hard and my legs shook—*be still, my beating heart.* But it beat so fast, I thought I might die. I turned and ran in the other direction, taking the fastest, longest strides of my life. My lungs burned. I sprinted well out of range, then bent double and wheezed.

Friday, September 10th

The brown car was waiting by the curb again today. This time, I walked right up to it. Don't ask me how I had the nerve. I just did. The passenger window was rolled down, and I leaned into it on my elbow. "Looking for Sasha?" I said.

Kevin did a double take. He didn't move, but his eyes bugged, and then he laughed. It sounded more like a bark. "Natalie! What's up?"

"Not much. You know, back to school, rah rah rah."

"Hop in."

"I don't think so."

"Why not?"

"Last I heard, you had your license suspended."

For a second, he winced, like I'd slapped him. Then he sneered. "Sasha said you turned into a suck—I guess she was right."

"Just 'cuz I'm not a shoplifter or a drunk driver, suddenly I'm a suck? Try again."

He blew out a puff of air, felt his pockets, and found a pack of cigarettes. He flicked it open. It was empty, and he tossed it on the floor. I was getting a cramp in my lower back from leaning forward, and besides, I felt self-conscious with my butt sticking out as kids streamed past. I stood up and noticed a dent on the roof of the car.

"Nat!"

"What?"

He mumbled something too low to hear. I was torn between wanting to run like I did yesterday, and wanting to get into the car where I could hear him. As I stood there trying to decide, he called my name again. This time his voice sounded gentle. I looked both ways, pulled the door open, and slid into the passenger seat.

"Let's get out of here," I said. "I don't want people looking at us."

He started up the car.

"Let's just go to Cattle Point," I said.

We drove in silence and parked overlooking the ocean. We watched the gulls and the waves. Finally he said, "That didn't go as well as I hoped."

"What do you mean? Were you looking for me?"

He twisted his hands on the steering wheel. "Not exactly. I mean, I thought we would run into each other eventually." He glanced at me. "I've thought about it quite a bit."

I squirmed in my seat. "So what's up with you? Whose car is this?"

"It's my buddy's. We sort of share it."

"Does he know you don't have a license?"

Kevin sighed. "He's okay with it."

"What if you got pulled over?"

"I'm not going to get pulled over." He unrolled his window.

"Even my mom gets pulled over sometimes! She spaces out and doesn't notice she's going through a school zone. If that happens, you're going to get your friend into a lot of trouble. You'll be up the creek too, of course."

Maybe I *was* starting to sound like a mouthpiece for the Law-Abiding Citizens' Association. The truth was, Kevin made me feel defenseless: I craved his touch, his kiss, his skin. If I acted bitchy, he couldn't tell how weak I was. "What happened to riding your bike?"

"It got stolen."

"Then you should walk or take the bus." I couldn't quit. "What are you *doing* with yourself, anyway?"

"I'm getting by. I'm helping a friend with his business." He patted the dashboard. "That's why we share the car."

Kevin didn't seem like the type to have entrepreneur friends. I couldn't really see him palling around with software designers or restaurant managers and applying for grants from the Ministry of Small Businesses. His black curls were looking a bit matted, he hadn't shaved in a while, and he wore a hemp necklace. In the next breath, I smelled a familiar aroma: weed.

"It's not legal. Sharing the car, I mean."

Kevin shook his head. "You seem to think the law is some ultimate authority on right and wrong. But it's not! The law is just something made up by some fat middle-aged guys in suits. Ever seen the Parliament channel on cable? They're like a bunch of overgrown kids picking on each other on the playground. And the worst part is that the laws don't benefit people. They benefit corporations."

Kevin must have made some new counter-culture friends. I wasn't up to an argument about the legal system. But I did have another burning question. "The last time we talked on the phone, you said you wanted to see me."

Kevin glanced at me. "Yeah?"

"When I was in Vancouver."

"I remember."

I looked away. I couldn't bring myself to ask, *What for?*

He opened the car door. "Let's get out."

Breathing fresh air and scrambling over rocks sounded good. I hauled my backpack with me so I wouldn't have to return to the car.

We found a bench at the top of the outcropping. He sat down and stretched his arms across the seat back. I had to choose a spot at the far end of the bench so that his arm wouldn't drape behind my shoulders. The wind buffeted us.

"This has been hard," he said, staring at the water.

"What do you mean?"

"We had an intense week in July." His forehead wrinkled. He hesitated, then said, "You've got something, Nat. You've got some ... some drive or sense of purpose or something. You've got this strength and ... and this sort of calmness to you. You're the calm in the eye of the storm." He looked at me. The wind swirled and eddied as if on cue. "I need to be around that sometimes. My life is just the opposite; it's one storm after another. You know?"

I can't believe he sees me that way. It's like he looks up to me, even though I'm so much younger.

"Does this mean you weren't just using me in the summer? Remember, you said, 'Older guys are only after one thing'?"

"Nat, that's what I mean: I don't really *feel* any older than you."

Monique said the same thing, and she's twenty-two, so maybe he's telling the truth.

We sat there for a little while longer, then I said I had to go.

"Can I give you a ride?"

I stood and hoisted my heavy pack onto my back. "No, thanks. I could use the walk."

He looked up at me from the bench. "Can I call you?"

His eyes pleaded, and I felt a surge of tenderness. "Okay."

As I plodded home, I thought about what he'd said. His feelings for me seemed genuine. And he'd made an effort to find me. I mean, he must have known Sasha was at Vic High. If he wasn't looking for me, why else would he park outside my school?

Saturday, September 11th

The owner of the corner store bagged the vanilla yogurt I'd biked down for at Mom's request—it would top the fruit salad she was making for lunch. He was handing me change when Sasha sauntered in, wearing flip-flops, cutoffs, and a scoop-necked T-shirt that drew attention to her breasts. Her makeup looked heavy enough for the stage. I was starting to speak when her eyes slid off me. She pretended not to know who I was.

"A pack of DuMauriers, please." Her voice had dropped half an octave into an "I-could-care-less" kind of drawl.

The proprietor jerked his thumb towards a sign next to the cash register: *It is illegal to sell tobacco to anyone under nineteen years of age.* "Need to see your ID."

"Come on, I buy cigarettes here all the time. It's usually your daughter who works Saturdays, right?"

The man tensed his jaw. "It's against the law to sell tobacco to minors. All cashiers working here know this. If not, who do you think gets fined?" He poked himself in the middle of his chest with his index finger. "I get fined. No ID, no cigarettes."

I edged towards the door. "Let's go, Sasha."

She slapped out of the store, and I followed her. She flipped her middle finger behind her head as we crossed the threshold. "I came all the way here because his daughter sold me a pack last week."

"You probably got her in trouble just now."

She snorted. "Not my problem." She blew air out her bottom lip to lift her bangs off her forehead. "That was my last chance. Now I'll have to break down and ask my brother for smokes."

"Or you could quit."

She singed me with her glare.

I looped the plastic grocery bag onto my handlebars. I wanted to get away, but I wanted to hear her say more about Kevin. "So what's new?"

"I have to stay at Vic High."

"Shitty," I said. "For the whole year?"

"For the fall, anyway," she said. "It's okay, though. The classes are a joke and the kids aren't as snotty. You know the rich kids at Oakridge, the ones who call themselves the Beautiful People? I found out they're only there because they were too dumb to pass the entrance exams at the private schools—all their daddies' cash couldn't make up for the fact that they're, like, brain-dead. No one would fall for their bullshit at Vic High."

A car pulled into a spot right beside the bike rack and we moved away from the exhaust. "Do you want to push our bikes for a ways?"

She checked her watch. "Okay, for a little ways."

We headed for the crosswalk. "How's it going with your family?" I said.

"Don't ask."

"Still not talking to your mom?"

"I want nothing to do with her."

I pressed the button to change the light.

"What about your dad?"

"He's putting a roof over my head. That's it. And I'd 'better be grateful I'm not in juvie.'"

"Sounds tense."

"Yeah." She used a high, strangled voice to underline the point. "He pretty much wishes me and my brother were never born."

At the mention of Kevin, my stomach jumped. Should I tell her I'd hung out with him the day before? I dreaded her anger, but keeping secrets again felt worse. The light changed and the two-tone walk signal chimed. "I saw Kevin yesterday."

"What? Where?"

I rolled my bike off the curb. "He was parked outside the school, so I went and talked to him." Oncoming pedestrians forced us to walk single file. I imagined her glowering at my back. On the opposite sidewalk, we fell in line again, shoulder-to-shoulder. "I guess he's driving without a license."

She stopped walking. "So? What's it to you?"

I didn't really have an answer to that. "I was just surprised he would take that kind of risk."

"You're such a suck. Why don't you just mind your own business?"

I hung my head and didn't reply.

Her voice changed as she realized the truth. "You're still obsessed with him, aren't you? That's what this is about. I can't fuckin' believe it. Trust me, you're not going to get anywhere with him."

The day before at Cattle Point, Kevin showed real emotion.

The feelings between us weren't one-sided. I was sure of it. "How do you know?"

Sasha laughed. "Believe me, I know. I've been fielding phone calls from his exes for years. Some of them were really nice girls, Nat. And pretty too." She swung her leg over her bike. "He made them all feel *special*." She tilted her head. "I'm going this way." She swooped into the road and did a donut. When she passed me again, she paused, her toe touching the curb. "You know what?"

I was adjusting my helmet. "What?"

"When you started this thing with Kevin, you obviously didn't care how I felt. So it's karma."

"What do you mean?"

"Getting hurt by Kevin. That's your karma."

She wheeled again and took off up the hill.

Sunday, September 12th

Dad called tonight to drop the bomb: he and Vi are getting married.

I didn't say congratulations. I said, "Does this mean you're staying in Ontario forever?"

From the upstairs phone, Paige asked, "Will you have babies?"

Dad hedged. I thought he was just too embarrassed to explain his vasectomy to Paige, so I said, "Dad had an operation so he can't have any more children." I expected Dad to back me up, but he didn't. "Right, Dad?"

He cleared his throat. "Um, well, uh ..." Usually, he's straight and to the point, very "business communications." So I knew something was up.

"The operation might actually be reversible."

"*What?*"

"I'm not saying we're going to have any children, but, well, Vi *has* asked me to consider reversing my operation."

"And you're *going* to?" I was practically shouting.

"I'm going to *consider* it, yes."

"Does that mean I'm going to have a little baby sister or brother?" Paige said from the bedroom. "Sweet! I've always wanted one."

She thinks it's like getting a goldfish or something. But I have a younger sibling. I know what it means. I'll feel responsible for those kids, my half-brothers or sisters, the way I do for Paige. What if something happens to Dad and Vi? There I'll be, the old-enough-to-be-their-mother half-sister. They'll rely on me. And Dad's acting like this has nothing to do with me!

My hands were shaking as I hung up, and my body temperature plummeted. I boiled water for tea, my teeth chattering.

Mom actually sounded excited. "Getting married!" Or maybe it was only surprise. She has a perma-flush these days, so I couldn't tell whether she was glowing in reaction to the news or not. How long does infatuation usually last? It'll be nice to have my mother back once she recovers.

Paige skipped downstairs and sprang into the kitchen. "I can't wait to be a bridesmaid!"

I pulled the afghan off the couch and drew it around me like a shawl. "The bride usually asks her friends, or her sisters, not the groom's daughters."

"You never know." Mom frowned at me and turned to Paige. "It's very possible that you two will be in the wedding party. And even if you're not, you'll be guests of honor."

I was still shivering, and my stomach felt hollow. Mom was making me feel like Natalie-the-Selfish-Grouch, who ruins everything for Paige. So I didn't say, "I don't want to go to the wedding." Instead, I sipped my tea and burnt my tongue.

I really hope the doctors can't reverse the vasectomy, or that Vi can't get pregnant. I know: I'll research infertility hexes. A wedding must be the perfect place to cast one.

Monday, September 13th

It was impossible to concentrate at school today. Burning sensations erupted in my chest every time I thought of Dad and Vi. During a Math quiz, I fell back into an old habit. I flipped my quiz over and wrote:

> *Dear Dad,*
> *How can you even THINK of starting another family? You have no right! You're totally absent from my life! If they made you take a parenting exam, you'd FAIL. It should be ILLEGAL for you to bring any more children into the world.*

I didn't notice the teacher patrolling the rows. My rapid writing must have caught his attention because he leaned over my desk. I flipped the paper, but not before he read part of it. How embarrassing. I erased the note once he moved on but left most of the quiz blank.

Even though Math isn't my strong suit, it's not like me to fail a test. After everyone left, I approached the front of the room. The teacher was stuffing the quizzes into his briefcase. He's kind of gruff, and I didn't know what to expect.

"Mr. Lee …"

He paused to look at me. His round, silver-rimmed glasses were slipping down the low bridge of his nose. "Yes?"

"I was wondering if I could rewrite the quiz. I—I couldn't concentrate today."

He smiled. "Don't worry about it. I won't hold one off-day against you."

Tuesday, September 14th

Off-Day #2. Crushing sadness. If I had a choice, I would pick anger: at least it gives me energy. Today, I slumped at my desk, shoulders rounded and chest caved in. My eyes kept filling with tears as I pretended to take notes.

> *Dear Dad,*
> *I've tried so hard not to miss you. I've tried so hard not to care. I'm tired of hoping and waiting. You don't love me. You never will.*

From the board, the Bio teacher took in my glassy stare; he probably thought I'd smoked weed at lunch. But I was low, not high. After class, I dragged myself down the hall like there were ten-pound weights in my shoes.

Wednesday, September 15th

School's not the same without Sasha.

Quitting Dance-Is has left a big hole in my life.

Kevin has vanished.

Mom has changed.

And now Dad is leaving us behind—again.

After dinner, I went to my room and pulled out a pad of paper. I needed to get it all out once and for all.

Dear Dad,
Weddings are supposed to be joyful, and I wish I felt happy
for you and Vi. But I don't.

There are things I've wanted to tell you for a long time,
and I can't hold them back anymore. Here goes. I wish you
didn't live so far away and that I got to see more of you. I
wish I didn't always have to be the one to phone. It makes
me feel like I don't matter to you. Even when I visit you, I
feel much less important to you than your work. You haven't
been around to see me grow up and it makes me very sad.
I miss you.

Now that you're marrying Vi, I'm scared I'll see you even less.
I'm scared you'll have other kids and give them the love and
attention I should have received. You'll never leave Ontario
and you'll forget about Paige and me.

I want the disappointment to end and the pain to stop.

I quit writing when a teardrop rolled off my cheek and landed
splat on the page. It was so long since I'd written to Dad. I gave
up trying to reach him years ago. As I re-read the letter, I cried
harder, knowing I would never send it. It was hopeless trying to
speak to him from the heart.

Mom knocked. "Nat? Are you all right?"

I blew my nose in response.

"Can I come in?"

"If you want." I must have sounded pathetic.

I let her read the letter, and she hugged me. "I'm sorry for all
of this hurt." She rocked me in her arms. "But, Nat, one thing is

for sure: your father loves you and Paige very much." It felt as if she'd hugged me again when she said that. I tried to ignore the voice inside that grumbled: *cliché, bullshit.*

It would have been better if Mom stopped there, but she continued. "When he doesn't call you or spend time with you, I know it's hard, but you have to try not to take it personally. He's a workaholic and, unfortunately, he doesn't properly appreciate the value of human relationships."

Anger flared up again and I pulled away. "But that's my point! How can he think of bringing more children into the world when he doesn't value the ones he already has?"

She shook her head and stared at the carpet, then lifted her chin. "All I can think is that making a commitment to Vi has changed him. That they're moving from a dating phase into more of a family phase." She reached to tuck my hair behind my ear, something she hasn't done since I was a kid. "You and Paige might actually benefit from it, you know. They dropped everything to come and see you dance in Vancouver, didn't they?"

"Uh-huh." I wasn't convinced, but I'd moped enough for one night.

"Why don't we make a batch of brownies?" Mom said.

"Did I hear someone say *brownies*?" Paige popped her head into my room. She has a sixth sense when it comes to chocolate. "I want to help!"

I closed the pad of paper and set it on my desk. "When you say, 'help,' you mean, 'lick the bowl,' right?" I tousled Paige's hair and she ducked out from under my hand.

By the time I brought a plate of brownies and a glass of milk back to my room, my letter-writing mood had passed. I tucked the pad away in my bottom drawer.

Thursday, September 16th

Every time I leave school, I scan the cars at the curb. If there's a brown one, my heart palpitates. I don't particularly *want* Kevin hunting me down after school. That's why I told him to call me. But I don't enjoy having a minor panic attack every time the phone rings either. I never know where he's staying or how to reach him. There's nothing to do but wait.

Friday, September 17th

The girls played grass hockey in PE today. We had to run up and down a muddy field with big wooden sticks, chasing a ball and blocking each other. I don't mind the idea of hitting balls—golf, tennis, ping pong, croquet—these are all civilized games. But why divide a class into enemy camps and make them charge at each other?

The teacher assigned us to teams and positions. Jamie played offensive forward on my side. Claire, a fullback, opposed us. My position—left wing—no doubt had to do with my size (small) and ability (poor). I faced off against Sara, a red-haired girl about my height and weight. When the ball finally came our way, I accidentally whacked her on the shins, really hard. There weren't enough shin pads to go around, and she wasn't wearing any. She yelped and my stomach turned. The teacher ran up, followed by Jamie and other attackers.

"I'm so sorry! I'm so sorry! Are you okay?" I said.

Sara was hopping on one leg, her face drawn in pain.

The teacher said, "Don't apologize. It's part of the game."

Jamie thumped her stick on the ground. "It's *our* team you have to worry about, not the other guys."

The teacher blew the whistle and everyone swarmed off

before I could respond. Even Sara limped away.

I cannot *believe* I am being taught to *physically harm* people and not feel bad about it. Did I accidentally sign up for *military* school? Are we in training for the battlefield? Whack someone on the other team today; kill someone from the Middle East tomorrow?

At the end of class, the teacher reminded us that we needed to either sign up to teach a class or choose a paper topic by the end of next week. Claire eyed me from the other side of the field, but I pretended not to see.

She caught up to me as I was ducking out of the change room. I was still shaken up, and as we left the school I told her what had happened. "I was forced to be violent! It goes against my beliefs. Maybe I can launch a protest. I conscientiously object to grass hockey!"

Claire's cheeks quivered. It looked like she was suppressing a smile.

"I should have known you wouldn't understand!" I scissored my legs to outstrip her. "You probably like spiking the volleyball into people's faces. It probably gives you a thrill."

Claire sped up and grabbed my arm. "Slow down a sec."

I looked back at the school. The grass hockey field was receding into the distance. I relaxed my pace.

"You're making a good point," she said, "but I'm the only one hearing it. Don't you think some of the other kids in the class might be feeling the same way? What about the girl you hit?"

"Sara." I stuffed my hands into the pockets of my hoodie. "She's going to have a massive bruise."

"Right. Sara is probably thinking she hates sports too. But, unlike you, she might be thinking that she hates being active

altogether because team sports are all she's ever been exposed to."
Claire twisted her upper body to face me as we walked, her arms
raised and her hands splayed. "Don't you think people like Sara
deserve to know about other types of physical activity? Don't you
think Sara deserves a dance lesson?" As we reached an intersection, kids waiting to cross the street turned their heads at her
raised voice.

It was my turn to choke back a laugh. "Since when did you
hire a speech writer?"

Claire dropped her arms and slapped the sides of her legs.
"How'd I do?"

The light changed, and we crossed. "Pretty good. But I don't
feel ready to teach. I'm not confident enough in myself to encourage other people."

"I can see the obituary now." She spread her hands in the air
as if framing a billboard: "After an unfortunate incident in her
Grade 10 PE class, Sara chose a life of inactivity. This led to her
untimely death. If only she had stayed active, she might still be
alive today. Instead of flowers, please send donations to the Y."

I laughed. Claire must have been born confident. My inse-
curities carried no weight with her. "You really are playing dirty,
my friend."

"Besides, Nat, you don't have to face the class alone. We'll do
it together—that's the whole idea."

I agreed to think about it on one condition: *she* had to consider taking classes with me at Eastside. We shook hands on it.

Lance starts teaching next week. Maybe he will inspire me.

Wednesday, September 22nd

Kevin finally called. "Are you free on Friday night?" He might have been a skydiving instructor shouting *Jump!* while I huddled inside a plane. The receiver slipped in my hand. My heart pounded. I swallowed and said, "Yes."

After I hung up, the adrenaline wore off and crabbiness set in. At dinner, Mom asked if I would babysit on Friday.

"I have plans."

She looked super disappointed. Apparently, Marine has a piece of art in a group show that opens in Nanaimo this weekend. "I promised to be there."

I gripped my fork and knife. "You should have checked with me before you made promises."

Paige spoke up. "You don't need to worry. *I* have plans too."

Guilt tugged at me for acting like Paige was a burden. Mom's face mirrored how I felt.

"I'm having a sleepover at Jessica's."

"That's great, honey!" Mom squeezed Paige's shoulder. "That'll give you a chance to use your new overnight suitcase, the one that Vi bought for you."

I wish she'd left Vi out of it. The mention of her name soured my mood even more. I pushed my chair back from the table.

"Aren't you going to finish your lasagna?" Mom said.

"I'm not hungry."

From the kitchen, I overheard Mom filling Paige in about teenagers, hormones, and moodiness. Ha. If she only knew.

Thursday, September 23rd

Today was my first day of modern class.

Lance faced us at the front of the studio. A short, sixty-year-old man in forest green sweat pants and bare feet, he pressed his shoulders back like a matador's, lengthened his spine, and held his head high.

He told us how to carry ourselves. "Imagine your line of vision as a searchlight that pierces the dark and reaches all the way to the horizon." Like a superhero with X-ray eyes, he swiveled his head at a slow, even pace.

In between exercises, he told stories. The life lessons went right over the head of some of the girls, but I ate them up. "Everyone has passion when they're young, but so many people get red lights, whether from teachers or parents or even from other kids. The spirit is tender and easily crushed by ridicule and rejection. People say, 'You have to develop a thick skin,' like it's a necessary life skill. But what happens to sensitivity when you thicken your skin? What happens to passion? They get buried. You see so many people on the bus, behind the counter at the store, and they're just going through the motions. They're dead behind the eyes, they've stopped truly living years before. And you wonder, who could that person be if they'd been given green lights instead of red?"

Lance teaches in order to shine a green light—the opposite of Ms. Kelly. All those years of her bootcamp-style instruction didn't strengthen me; they just built up my defenses. Now, my confidence is slowly growing from the inside out. Lance still corrects us—he believes in precision—but I don't leave his class doubting my self-worth, the way I often used to do. In his class, we dance to celebrate movement. We've been given beautiful instruments—our bodies—and now we are learning to play.

When I got home from Lance's class tonight, Claire called to find out my decision about teaching, since tomorrow's the deadline. "Okay," I said. "I give in. But you better do most of the talking!"

Friday, September 24th, night, pre-date

Mom approached me after school today when I was fixing my afternoon snack. Paige was packing her overnight bag upstairs. Mom asked how I would feel if she stayed overnight in Nanaimo tonight.

My guts seized up.

"It's only because Paige is going to be at a sleepover, otherwise I wouldn't ask." She looked worried. "I really don't like crossing the Malahat in the dark. I was going to do it anyway, but they're predicting rain. That means there'll be a terrible glare on the road. I would feel so much safer getting a motel room."

I couldn't blame her for not wanting to drive at night over the mountain north of Victoria: The highway is narrow, winding, and unlit. But her plan stressed me out. "Can't you get a ride with Marine?"

"She's staying over too." Mom blushed and added, "The curator is putting her up."

I didn't want to have the house to myself. Not on a night when I was going out with Kevin for the first time in six weeks. I didn't want the responsibility. Parents are supposed to be there as a buffer so you don't have to face situations you're not ready to handle. My God! Didn't she learn that the last time?

She was looking at me with such a hopeful expression, like *I* was the parent and she was asking permission.

"Let me think about it."

She backed up a few steps and bumped into the table. "Sure. Take your time." She crossed the room, moved a mug from the dish rack to the cupboard, turned in a circle, and fell to sorting the mail.

I considered my options as I chopped celery and sliced cheddar cheese:

1) Say *No, I'm not comfortable staying on my own*, and have Mom miss the art show and mope around, lovesick and frustrated. Or, worse, have her drive late at night over the Malahat, hit a deer, and total Kermit.

2) Say *Yes*, have the house to myself, and be taken advantage of by Kevin.

I forgot what I was doing and sliced almost the whole block of cheese. Considering Option 2 made me break out in a nervous sweat. Should I cancel my date and stay home alone? That didn't seem fair either. I packaged up the extra cheese and replaced it. The fridge door smacked and I spun around, inspired:

3) Say *Yes*, and not let Kevin *know* that I have the house to myself.

Ah yes. The Third Way!

"Okay, Mom."

She dropped a stack of envelopes on the floor just as Paige wheeled her new bag into the kitchen. Mom bent over to pick up the mail and when she straightened, the blood had rushed to her head. "Honey, I'm going to stay over in Nanaimo tonight." She sounded a little out of breath.

Paige searched my face. "So Nat will be here all by herself!"

A sob caught in my throat. How could Mom be so oblivious when Paige empathized right away?

"That's not very fun," Paige continued. "Too bad *you're* not having a sleepover, Nat."

I tried to reassure them. But why *have* we gone our separate ways again so soon? What happened to family night on Friday, with pizza and a video? Would it be any different if Paige and I were living with Dad and Vi, a normal couple, rather than with a woman going through her second adolescence at forty-two?

2:00 a.m.

I can't fucking believe it. Going to shower.

Saturday, September 25th, morning, Con Brio

Biked here at 7:30 a.m. It didn't open till 8 a.m. Manager eyed me suspiciously when he opened up. Probably thought I was a street kid who'd been loitering there all night.

Sipping latte. Warm. Medicinal.

Where to start?

Does it matter? Is there any point reflecting on all this stuff? I thought I was changing, I thought I was gaining control of my life. Then I repeat the same damn mistakes. Well, not exactly the same.

The evening started okay. Bussed to meet Kevin at the house where he's staying. He came to the door and asked me if I wanted to go for a walk. "My roommate's home." I couldn't tell whether we were giving the roommate his privacy, or seeking our own. We cut across the street to a small neighborhood park. Kevin led the way to the playground. He gestured like a butler to the equipment: "See-saw, madam?"

We teetered back and forth for a while, and then he planted his butt on the ground and trapped me up high. Because he's so much heavier, I couldn't get down. He smirked and chewed grass. When I demanded that he let me down, he faked a move to get up all at once, which would have made me crash to the ground. My stomach curled in fear. That was it.

I twisted my head, gauged the five-foot drop, gripped the seat with my hands, and flung myself backwards. I landed on my feet and staggered only a bit before I stormed to the water fountain. Kevin ran after me. "Sorry, Nat! It was only a joke."

I leaned over the drinking fountain, cranked the handle, filled my mouth with water, and spat at him.

"Hey!" He jumped backwards and pulled his spattered T-shirt away from his body. He looked stunned, but shook himself out of it. "Are we *even* now?"

I pursed my mouth. "We'll see."

Back at the house, his roommate (and boss?), the owner of the little brown car, was sunk in an armchair watching Japanese cartoons. I asked if he understood Japanese, and he shook his head, then a grin split his face. "Doesn't matter." He had a couple of dead teeth.

He asked if we wanted to smoke a bowl. I shook my head but Kevin said sure, then offered me a beer. I didn't want to be called a "suck" again, so I accepted a bottle. We watched the cartoon until I started to zone out, maybe from the secondhand smoke.

"What do you think, Nat, want to go clubbing?"

I raised my eyebrows at him. *I'm fifteen, remember?*

"You can see how the nightlife here compares to Vancouver."

"When I was in Vancouver, I borrowed someone's ID."

"Don't worry, we have a VIP pass, we'll get you in."

I hadn't dressed for a night on the town, but in the bathroom, I reapplied lipstick, knotted my shirt at the waist to show a little belly, and teased my hair. My mind raced. Hadn't I made some vow to myself? Right: no driving with Kevin since he doesn't have a license. I sipped my beer. That was illegal, too, at my age. I didn't much like the taste, but to call it "criminal" did seem harsh. As for going to a bar … I'd done it in Vancouver. It didn't seem too dangerous, as long as I went with people I knew. I communed with my mirror image: *Okay. You can have a drink or two, and you can go to a bar. But I draw the line at getting into a car with an unlicensed driver.*

I squared off my shoulders and took a deep breath. I had to tell Kevin I wouldn't go with him. I opened the bathroom door and walked down the hall to the living room.

Kevin was slouching against the doorjamb. He checked out my belly and smiled. "Ready to go?"

"Look—" I began.

Kevin's roommate brushed past him into the front hall. He pushed his bare feet into a pair of flip-flops.

"Jeremy's going to drive us," Kevin said.

The roommate pulled a key chain off a hook by the front door and shook it, like a bell, beside his face. "Don't worry," he said. "I've got a license."

It was a short drive downtown. Jeremy pulled into the taxi zone right outside the club. "Have fun, kids." He and Kevin shook hands in a loose, arm-wrestling hold. When I stepped out of the car, people standing in line turned to look. Twenty-something girls flung ironed-straight hair over their bare shoulders. Guys scuffed the ground and spat as we passed. Kevin headed straight for the entrance. The bouncer nodded at the VIP pass, flicked his eyes over my face, and didn't ask for ID. Inside, darkness and a steady beat engulfed us.

Kevin bought me a piña colada. Its creamy pineapple and coconut taste disguised the alcohol, and I downed it fast. He chuckled and bought me another. Every so often, someone approached him and shook hands. They would dip their hands into their pockets and shake again. Either he had touchy-feely friends, or it was some kind of ritual. I didn't have long to ponder it. With the heat of the liquor in me, the old feelings welled up, and I wanted him to myself. I pulled him onto the dance floor on a slow song. We held each other close and kissed. After the song ended, we found a dark corner and made out some more. We surfaced from a kiss at one point, and he said, "What time are you supposed to be home?"

I gave him a blank look, then remembered: he didn't know Mom wasn't home. "Midnight or so."

He checked his watch. "Bad news, we're going to have to get going. Just as well, 'cause I was about to drink our cab fare."

I'd never taken a cab before. It was weird to have a stranger chauffeur us around. The wide back seat, upholstered in red velvet, bounced underneath us as we drove. Kevin's hand rested on my thigh. As we pulled to the curb in front of my house, he said, "Looks like your mom's out."

Damn the carport. If we had a covered garage, he would never have known her car wasn't there. Before I knew what was happening, Kevin pulled a wad of bills out of his jeans pocket, unfolded a couple, and paid the driver. I was wondering why he carried so much loose cash in his pockets when it occurred to me: the strange handshakes in the nightclub weren't greetings. They were sales transactions. He was dealing!

The yellow taxi streaked off in a trail of exhaust fumes.

"Is your sister in there with a babysitter, or what?"

I wanted to be strong, but he nuzzled my neck. His mouth and the alcohol crushed my resolve. I spilled the truth and soon we were back where we left off a month ago, only this time in my bed, not in Mom's.

Fooling around felt good, but when things reached the crucial point I said, "Stop. No, we can't do this without a condom. Not again."

He rolled onto his back and expelled his breath at the ceiling. "I don't have one! I totally didn't expect this to happen tonight."

"Then we can't!"

"Come on, Nat, I'll be careful."

"What does that mean?"

He slid back on top of me. "I'll pull out."

"No."

He traced his finger down my belly. "But isn't this bliss?"

Bad choice of words! *Bliss* made me think of my dad and his hero quest, and that broke the spell. Kevin was using his hand to guide himself into me. I remembered the teeter-totter. I planted my palms on the mattress and shoved back off the bed. I stood and he knelt. We eyed each other. He had a burning, needy look that scared me. "Why are you being such a tease? We did this before."

The shock hit me first in the gut, then outlined my limbs, cold and separate. *We did this before.* I stared across the bed at this stranger. We made a *mistake* before, which I handled on my own. The worry, the nearly too-late trip to the drugstore, the long days of waiting for my period to come, the nasty tests at the clinic. I told him all this on the phone that night from Vancouver. He must have ignored what I said. He didn't care what the consequences were for me. My feelings meant nothing to him.

"It's no big deal after the first time, Natalie. It just gets better. Come on …"

He didn't learn from mistakes, but that didn't mean I couldn't.

I started to dress. He scooted across the bed and reached for my breast. I slapped his hand away. I was so turned off, nothing he could do would tempt me.

"I don't know why you're acting so frigid. It's not like we haven't done this before."

"Would you shut up? Would you just shut up and leave?"

By the time I was fully dressed, he saw that I meant it and switched tactics. "I'll stop bugging you, let's just lie down and go to sleep. Your mom's not coming back till tomorrow, and it's late."

I went to the kitchen, pulled out the phone book, found the number for a taxi, and dialed. He heard me on the phone and stumbled out of the bedroom. "Whoa, whoa, don't do that, you psycho bitch. Look at me, I'm up, I'm getting dressed. I don't have money for a cab."

I held the receiver to my chest. "What about all that money from your *customers*?"

"Jeremy fronted me that—ugh!" Kevin cut himself off. He swore as he buttoned his jeans.

The dispatcher was saying something. I put the phone to my ear. "Do you want to cancel the cab, ma'am?"

"I guess so. Thanks anyway."

Kevin shoved his feet into his shoes in the front hall.

"I don't know why you're doing this, Nat. But I know one thing for sure." He paused with his hand on the doorknob.

"You're going to regret it." He swung the door open and slammed it behind him.

I shuddered. What did he mean by that? Was he going to come back and set fire to the house? Round up his friends and gang rape me? Or what? Maybe he just meant, "One day when I'm rich and famous, you'll be sorry you let me slip through your fingers." The fact is, I don't know him well enough to interpret his tone, and that's a sad thing to have to admit about your first lover.

I lay in bed, rigid, and waited for daylight. I left the house as soon as I could. Now I'm wired on latte.

At least I don't have to make another trip to the drugstore. I need more water. And I'm going to need sleep.

Later

The house was still standing when I returned, so I guess whatever else Kevin is, he's not an arsonist. Inside, the silence surprised me. The day had no right to be so young. I wanted to nap, but not in my bed, the scene of Kevin's and my final standoff.

In the living room, the couch sagged underneath me. Saturday morning cartoons reminded me of the previous night's cartoon-and-bong show, and I shut them off. An afghan, crocheted by my grandma, lay at my feet. I hitched it up to my shoulders and hugged myself. Kevin had probably only called me in the first place because he needed a date for camouflage at the club. And, when I saw him waiting at the school—he wasn't looking for me; he was dealing there, too! I was such an idiot.

Outside the window stood a cedar hedge, heavy with rainwater. Each time a drop fell from one branch to the next, green fronds shook with the weight. Drip, quiver … drip, quiver … drip …

I must have drifted off, because the ringing of the phone woke me up.

I was so tired, my stomach forgot to clench with the usual fear that it might be Kevin.

"G'morning, g'Nat."

"Hi." Was I hallucinating? "Dad?"

"How are you?" he said.

"I've been better. But I've also been worse."

Dead air. I'd forgotten to echo Dad's "How are you?" Who made up these stupid rules for conversation, anyway?

"I—I got your letter."

"*What?* What letter? What do you mean?"

"You haven't written me that many letters in the past while. In fact, I can't remember when I got the last one. So it's, you know, the only letter you've written in recent memory."

I sat up. The afghan tangled itself around my legs. I balled it up and threw it to the floor. "*I didn't mail that letter!*"

More dead air.

"So this is Denise's doing, is it?"

"I'll kill her!"

"Take a few deep breaths."

"Dad, stay on the line for a minute." I dropped the phone on the sofa, ran to my room, and yanked open my bottom desk drawer. The pad of paper was sitting right where I'd left it. Dad had to be mistaken. I lifted the cover. The top sheet was blank. I bent down and made out faint indentations: *Dear Dad . . .*

I zombie-walked back to the living room and picked up the receiver. "I'm back." I stared out the window at the cedar hedge.

"I did think it was strange that you didn't sign it," he said.

"I don't even remember what I wrote."

Trust Dad to call when I was raw and defenseless from lack of sleep and the whole Kevin thing. "This is really taking me by surprise."

Dad's voice got quieter. "I can see that. I had no idea you didn't mail it yourself."

I was about to say, "Let's just forget this ever happened." But something exploded, and I let it rip. "No, Dad, I stopped mailing you letters because you never fucking wrote back."

He cleared his throat. "Right, that's in line with what you say here, in the letter. Look, Natalie, I'm glad this letter got to me, however it happened, because it seems to me you've been really honest here."

"You're right. So you know what I think. What have *you* got to say?"

I heard a murmur in the background. "Did Vi read the letter?"

"I've shared it with her, yes, because of course it affects her."

"How *can* you think of having more kids when you don't parent the ones you have? Huh? What's your answer to that?"

"Natalie, it's a fair question. That's my answer."

"You talk like every sentence is getting checked over by your lawyer first. Why can't you just speak from the heart? Do you *have* one?"

"Everything you're saying is—you're—you're not the only one to point these things out, Nat. Your mother, of course, but your mother and I weren't—I mean, my work—my workaholism wasn't the only problem between your mother and me."

"I'm not talking about that anymore, Dad, I mean, give me *some* credit, I'm not saying, *Boo-hoo, I want Mommy and Daddy back together again.* I'm not living in Never Never Land here. I'm just talking about, like, have you heard about the Deadbeat Dad laws?"

He bristled. "I have always sent my support payments, religiously; your mother—"

"I'm not talking about money, Dad, for God's sake, money is what you *do* give. I'm talking about time, attention, energy …" Damn it, I wouldn't censor myself this time. "I'm talking about *love*, Dad."

"Natalie, I do love you."

It was the first time Dad had said that to me. I breathed in: a tiny candle lit up inside my ribcage. I breathed out: anger flooded my chest cavity and doused the flame. "Well, it's *pretty* hard to tell sometimes."

He cleared his throat. "I can see what you mean, Nat, and that's why I wanted to tell you what we've been talking about since your letter came."

That shut me up. I'd written the letter to vent. I'd never planned to send it, so I hadn't even considered potential consequences. Now what?

"We see your point, we really do. Vi, especially, she said, if we try to start over without undoing past mistakes, we'll just repeat them all over again."

"Meaning?"

"Meaning, if she and I have a child, that child is probably going to grow up resenting me just as much as you do."

"Uh-huh." I still didn't see where this was going. "So?"

"So, we're thinking seriously about relocating. I can't give you an exact date, but we feel fairly certain that by late spring we'll be on the West Coast. Probably in Vancouver. You're right about everything. I've missed too much of your and Paige's childhoods already."

"I'm no longer a child, period."

"There you go." He hesitated. "The timing is good, now, with your mother and I both moving on in our lives."

"*You* know about Mom moving on? You and Mom really *are* opening up to each other these days. She hasn't even officially told *me* yet."

"She hasn't said anything, no. It was just an impression I got when we all spent time together in Vancouver."

I kept quiet for a few seconds. I was letting it all sink in.

"Are you saying you're going to move out here just because of my letter?"

"It's crossed our minds before, of course. I'm at a point where I'm ready for a change at work. And Vi really loves Vancouver. The visit last month just confirmed that." He paused. "But, yes, your letter kind of pushed us past the 'thinking about it' stage and into the planning stage."

Vi said something I couldn't make out.

"What did she say?"

"She said, 'into the Let's do it!' stage. And, there's something else you deserve credit for."

"Yeah?"

"The picnic at Stanley Park really made it concrete. It showed that we could all get along as a kind of extended family. So, thank you, Nat."

"You're welcome, I guess."

I hung up and flopped on the couch. Hand over hand, I pulled the afghan off the floor and tucked it around me.

The next thing I knew, Mom was calling out, "Hellooo! Anybody home?" Fresh air gusted from the open door.

"Morning," I croaked.

I restrained myself from confronting her about the letter. I wanted to hoard Dad's news, at least until I got some sleep and could think straight.

"I thought I would whip up some crepes and make a couple of fondues, one cheese and one chocolate, to dip fruit in. It can be a special brunch for when Paige gets home. Want to help?"

Spare me. "Maybe later."

"How was your date?"

I struggled to my feet and pulled the afghan around me. "Fine, thanks."

In the bathroom, I filled the tub with hot water and lowered myself in. The room steamed up. I was hiding inside a cloud.

Sunday, September 26th

Sun streamed into the kitchen this morning. In the yellow light, Paige washed the breakfast dishes. Mom had gone to the store. Even after thirteen hours' sleep, I was upset with Mom for mailing my letter. I was figuring out what to say to her as I dried the dishes and put them away.

"Earth to Natalie!" Paige said.

"What?"

"I just asked you a question."

"Oh. Sorry." I squeezed my fingers together, trying to reach into a drinking glass. The mouth was too narrow, so I poked the towel inside with the handle of a wooden spoon and swished it around. "What's the question?"

"I *said*, 'When do you want to phone Dad today?'"

"Ah, yes. It's 'Phone-Dad' day."

She passed me another glass, and I tried again to dry the inside. This time I managed to push my fingers in. The glass fit tight around the base of my hand.

"You can call him by yourself today."

Paige sharpened her voice. "Why?"

"Because ..." I didn't know how much to tell her. The glass clamped my hand, like a cast. "I talked to him yesterday."

"When?"

"He called in the morning, before you got home."

Paige turned on the tap to rinse suds off a plate. "What did he say?"

A surge of excitement made me blurt it out. "They're thinking of moving to Vancouver!"

Paige dropped the plate back into the water and grabbed my arm with sudsy hands. "Really? Then I'm so glad I sent him your letter."

"*You* sent it? *You* sent it? How could you?"

Her face fell, and she backed away until the counter divided us.

I struggled to free my hand from the glass. "I thought it must have been Mom. I was about to let her have it! Why did you do that?"

"I heard you crying that day, and I just thought Dad should know what you were feeling. He was always asking about you in the summer, you know. He really cares about you, and he felt sad that you were growing apart."

"He *said* that?"

"No, of course not. You know Dad. But I could tell." She let go of the counter and twirled. The varnished kitchen floor makes for killer pirouettes. "I'm so excited they're going to move out here! Aren't you?"

I finally pulled off the glass and flexed my fingers. "It might not even happen. And even if they do move, things might not change much." I faced the sink.

From behind me, Paige said, "What makes you so sad?"

Her question pierced me. I would have called myself a grouch, but she'd rooted out the source.

I pivoted and crossed my arms. "We've just missed out on so much. We can never get back those years with Dad. It's too late." I sighed. "At least, it's too late for me. My childhood is over."

Paige marched to the sink. "Just because we can't go back doesn't mean things can't get better!" She seized the plate she'd dropped, rinsed it, and passed it to me. "Things *are* getting better, I *know* they are." She washed on. Bowls, forks, saucers, and knives piled up in the rack. I worked hard to keep up. The sun shone so brightly, it seemed to help me dry.

Paige's determination won me over. Who was I to crush her hope? "You're right. It could work out really great." I clenched my jaw for dramatic effect. "So just this once I won't KILL you for taking my letter! You do realize that was a terrible invasion of my privacy, don't you?"

"Yeah. I'm sorry."

She hummed as she finished the dishes. Faces can't keep secrets in the morning light, and hers didn't look very regretful. When I caught my reflection in the window pane, I looked pretty pleased myself.

Monday, September 27th

When I left school today, something was missing. It took me a minute to figure out what. I walked past the line of cars in the pick-up and drop-off zone and felt—nothing. My heart didn't pound. My stomach wasn't churning. My palms weren't sweating, and my knees didn't shake. I didn't have to check for the brown Toyota. I knew Kevin wouldn't be back.

I took deep breaths of good-smelling, outdoor air. My lungs swelled. I spread my arms. I owned myself again. Freedom! How sweet it felt.

Saturday, October 2nd

When I pictured Claire and me in front of our PE class, it was obvious that pink tights and ballet-style leotards weren't going to help us "sell" dance to the masses. "Not to be shallow about this," I said to Claire on the phone, "but … what exactly are we going to wear?"

"Excellent question," she said. We were arranging to meet and plan the class. "We could always start with a little shopping to get us in the mood."

I needed new gear for my modern classes, anyway, so we bussed downtown to the trendy yoga store. The mannequins had been sawed in two like magicians' assistants. A row of upper halves sported various tops, from full-torso to skimpy-bikini style. Lining the opposite wall, the bottom halves modeled pants that ranged from flared to peg-leg and floor-length to cropped. I read a few price tags and whistled. "Let's try on a bunch and pick our favorites, then see how close a match we can find at the Bay and the second-hand store." (I gave silent thanks to Sasha for the strategy.)

The lineup for the change rooms belonged outside a washroom at a sold-out concert. We had to wait so long that I was about to suggest we forget it, when a familiar, dark-haired girl emerged from one of the change rooms, her arms piled high with clothing.

"Lisa!"

She scanned the row of shoppers, then her face broke into a smile. "Hi, Natalie! Hi, Claire!" She approached us. "How *are* you?"

I'd last seen Lisa on the emergency trip to the drugstore—the one only she and Kevin knew about. "Keeping out of trouble."

A change room opened up and Claire nudged me.

"You go ahead," I said.

Claire said, "Nice seeing you, Lisa," and disappeared behind a curtain.

I lowered my voice and leaned into my summer confidante. "Thanks for all your help with … you know. Everything. I got lucky, I guess."

"You did." She nodded. "I'm glad."

"You were right about Kevin. And I'm finally following your advice."

"You mean you're forgetting about him?"

"Trying to. It's not easy."

She touched my arm and smiled. "It never is."

I told her about Lance's class and urged her to take it.

"I just might." She raised her armful of clothes. "I've been doing yoga, but it's not the same. I miss moving across the room."

Claire stepped out to model a yellow top. The t-back showed off her strong upper body. Lisa and I gave her two thumbs up.

A couple of hours later, Claire and I had found affordable

outfits, but we still hadn't discussed our lesson plan. I was starting to panic as we ate lunch at a sidewalk café.

"By the time we finish eating and wait for the bus and get back home, we'll hardly have any time left before dinner to plan the class."

"Calm down!" Claire said. "You're going to give yourself indigestion. After we eat, let's go to the legislature lawn and block out the movement. We can write up our introduction tonight."

"The legislature lawn?" I said, meaning, *Are you out of your mind?*

"It's just down the street, it's public, and there's lots of space." Claire took a bite of her BLT. "Don't worry. It'll be perfect."

I sighed and spooned my chili. Why had I let her talk me into this in the first place?

Claire led the way down Government Street past the Inner Harbour. As the legislature lawn came into view, so did the mass of people occupying it. Just what we needed: a demonstration. "Let's go back to the bus stop." I turned around. The thought of teaching was stressing me out enough already. Political protesters were more than I could handle.

"It's okay, Nat. There's a back lawn we can use."

Claire did *not* know when to quit. "How do you know?"

"I was playing Frisbee on the front lawn with Jake this summer. A security guard came up to us and said it was fine if we played, but to please do it on the back lawn where we wouldn't bonk any tourists on the head."

"Are you sure? We can't afford to waste any time."

"Trust me. I want to get this figured out as much as you do."

We moved closer to the lawn. A podium at the front of the crowd held a microphone and loudspeakers. A reggae song by

Peter Tosh was playing. A few people waved flags covered in leafy, green plants. Others carried signs that read

Decriminalize Cannabis
Stop Arresting Medical Marijuana Providers
Free the Plant

The smell of weed wafted from more than one direction. A man mounted the podium and tapped the mic. I started. He looked familiar, and, without thinking, I lunged forward to get a closer look. As he adjusted the mic, someone shut off the music.

"Hello, all you wonderful people. My name is Jeremy, and I'm a pothead."

The crowd cheered, and the speaker's smile split his face. I was sure of it now: He was Kevin's roommate.

"We're gathered here today to make a public demand for the legalization of cannabis." More cheers.

"Nat?" Claire had followed me. "What on earth are you doing? I didn't see you take off."

I turned up one palm like a stop sign and signaled "Shh" with my other hand. My eyes didn't leave the stage.

Jeremy continued. "We're going to hear from a number of medical marijuana patients just how important this plant is for their day-to-day survival. We're also going to hear from a member of LEAD: Law Enforcement Asking for Decriminalization, a group of police officers who are speaking out against the War on Drugs."

I would *never* have expected the man who drove Kevin and me to the night club last week to address a crowd in front of the Parliament Buildings. He didn't look much different—I shifted until I could see his feet—he was even wearing the same flip-flops. But the setting made him seem important. A photographer squatted by the riser and snapped shots of Jeremy and the crowd. This event might appear in the paper. I turned around. In a semi-circle beyond the protestors, police officers were standing by. Despite the smell of weed, they kept their distance.

"I thought you were in a hurry," Claire said.

"Just a minute."

"Hey, there's Sasha!"

"Where?"

Claire pointed to the front of the crowd. "Let's go say hi."

"I don't know …"

But Claire was already weaving her way towards the podium. I followed. The emcee was wrapping up his introduction amidst applause as I reached the other girls. Claire stood between Sasha and me.

"What are you doing here?" Sasha said.

"We were just passing by," Claire said. "What are *you* doing here?"

"I'm collecting signatures. Want to sign?" She passed her clipboard to Claire, who started reading the petition.

"How did you get involved in this?" I asked. Sasha was wearing a T-shirt that was a couple of sizes too big. "LEGALIZE," it said. Beneath the black letters sprouted a huge green leaf.

"Jeremy's a friend of Kevin's," she said. "He asked if I wanted to help out, so I came down. Kev's here too." She looked past my shoulder, and I followed her gaze to the middle of the crowd. Kevin was holding a sign that said *Stop Arresting Responsible Marijuana Users*. A young woman had wedged herself right up against him, her breasts almost brushing his rib cage. She looked up at him and then dropped her eyelids. With his free hand, Kevin picked up a chain that hung around her neck and bent to look at it. If she'd tilted up her head, their lips would have met. My stomach twisted and I jerked away.

I expected Sasha to gloat, but she was watching Jeremy. He noticed her and winked. She smiled and tucked in her chin, suddenly bashful. *Uh-oh. That could be a dangerous crush.*

Claire had signed the petition. She tapped Sasha to get her attention and handed it back.

"Nat?" Sasha offered me the clipboard.

"It's about medical marijuana," Claire said.

"A bunch of people are about to tell their stories," Sasha said. "You should stay and listen." She focused on the stage.

My last experience in a crowd had been on Canada Day, when people had gathered for the fireworks and disbanded right away. These protesters seemed more closely knit. Maybe they gave Sasha and Kevin a sense of belonging.

Claire tugged on my sleeve and tilted her head towards the road. "Let's go," she mouthed. The next speaker had already begun.

I leaned across Claire and spoke into Sasha's ear. "It's really interesting, but we've got homework. Maybe another time."

Sasha shrugged. "Whatever."

Claire and I dodged our way back to the sidewalk.

"I'm not going to be able to concentrate with all that going on over here," I said.

Claire surprised me. "Me neither."

We bussed back to my place and planned our lesson in the yard.

Sunday, October 3rd

The revving of an engine woke me up this morning. It sounded like the car was in our driveway. I checked my bedside clock: 6 a.m. What the ...? I rolled over and pried the blinds apart. A hatchback was pulling out. It paused at the road, and the person driving rubbed their face, scrubbing sleep away. When they gripped the steering wheel again, I saw a woman's face: It was Marine. Slipping away at dawn. With bed head. I plopped back down, pulled up my quilt, and fell asleep.

This afternoon, Paige had a play date with Jessica. After Mom and I dropped her off, we walked along Dallas Road. The summer keeps stretching on this year, with endless hours of sunshine. The grass smelled sweet and dry, the wild roses still bloomed, and maple and oak leaves were just starting to turn yellow, orange, and brown. When two young women passed by holding hands, I took it as my cue.

"I heard Marine leave this morning."

Mom tensed up. "You did?"

"Her car woke me up."

"Sorry."

"It's okay. I fell back asleep."

We walked on in silence until a collie dog barked at Mom's ankles and circled her. She nearly tripped over its leash. The owner laughed unapologetically. I waited for Mom to disentangle herself. When we had a bit of sidewalk to ourselves, I carried on. "What I'm trying to say is, you two shouldn't have to sneak around. It's okay with me that you're dating her."

Mom blushed and stared at the ground. That's the beauty of broaching difficult subjects when you're walking. It's easy not to look at each other. And fresh air helps to dispel any tension. She didn't say anything for a long time. People streamed by.

Finally, during a break in the foot traffic, she said quietly, "How long have you known?"

"Remember that night you thought I was sleeping over at Sasha's, when you had Marine over? Paige had just left for Ontario?"

"That long!" She looked down again.

"I went to move the sprinkler and saw you two through the window."

"Oh …" she said. Then, with a start, "Oh!"

"That was my reaction too."

Her cheeks burned. "I'm sorry you had to find out that way, Natalie."

We passed the off-leash area where dogs bounded and ran. With so much variety in size, shape, and color, it was incredible that they belonged to the same species.

"It's not really all that shocking, you know. What's been hard is all the secrecy."

Mom nodded and folded her arms across her chest. "It's been very … difficult for me, the way I was raised. I wouldn't have chosen … to live this way, but, Marine is, well…. I feel very strongly about her."

I tried hard to think of Mom as Denise, a person with her own wants and needs. "You seem really happy, Mom. Distracted, but happy." I wanted to add: *So, I'm happy for you.* But something held me back. I bit my lip. "Mom, if you're—" I couldn't quite bring myself to say *a lesbian.* So I said, "—in love with Marine, does that mean you were never really in love with Dad?"

"No." She didn't hesitate. "It doesn't mean that. I was in love with your father, but we grew apart, and now all these years later, I've fallen in love again."

"With a woman."

"With Marine, who happens to be a woman."

The worry melted away: Paige and I had been born out of love, not out of a relationship my mother settled for because she was too scared to come out.

We were nearing the end of our walk by the time Mom asked about Kevin. All I said was, "I'm not going to see him anymore. He's too old for me."

"What a relief. That's what I always felt."

I stopped dead. "Why didn't you say so?"

She sighed and halted on the cliff, facing the sea with her hands on her hips. "I didn't want to be the heavy-handed author-ity figure forbidding you from doing things. That's how my parents acted with me. Overprotective. I figured it would just encourage you to rebel." She dropped her arms to her sides and looked at me. "I'm sorry if I let you down."

"It's okay. You didn't really."

Someday, I might tell her more about what happened with Kevin. For now, I'd rather put it behind me. Maybe I'll date someone else this year, someone my own age. But, frankly, I'm more interested in dance.

Wednesday, October 6th

We taught our Intro to Dance class in PE today. It wasn't easy to win over the jocks, especially the guys. They rolled their eyes when the teacher introduced us. "C'mon, man, it's soccer season. If we have to do a lame dance unit, can't it wait till winter, when the weather sucks anyway?" A rugby player pointed an index finger to the top of his head, tucked his free hand into his armpit, and twirled on the spot.

But when Claire marched to the front of the room in her yellow t-back top and black bike shorts, they quieted down. I tagged behind like a younger sister. How was I ever going to make it through the class?

Sara, the red-haired girl I'd whacked in the shins with my grass-hockey stick, was shifting from one foot to the other at the side of the room. She plucked the sides of her sweat pants as if they were too tight around the thigh. She rounded her shoulders and kept her eyes on the floor. It looked like she wanted to disappear. It dawned on me that I was *not* the most uncomfortable person in the room. Everything changed: I had something to give.

Claire said, "Listen up. We're not here to make dancers out of you. That would take a lot longer than one class. And, guys, we're not here to threaten your masculinity, either. All we want to do today is raise your level of body awareness."

She nodded at me. I took a breath and pitched in. "Body awareness will improve your performance in any sport." I forced myself to make eye contact with the jocks in the back row. "And it's the number one way to prevent injury. Most people spend hours every day ignoring their bodies, even when they're playing sports, but especially when they're sitting at a desk." I listed potential injuries. "If you increase your body awareness, you'll be alert to any discomfort or pain long before it becomes a problem."

We rolled out the DVD player to show a clip of modern dance soloist Margie Gillis. "Just look at how much physical control she has. Imagine what that would be like." The dancer articulated every square inch of her body. Her limbs moved so fluidly, they appeared to have lives of their own. When I turned from the screen, the class was absorbed, for the most part. I caught Claire's eye. *It's working!*

With the video as inspiration, Claire and I took turns leading movement from the front. The other circulated and made comments one-on-one. By the end of the lesson, the whole class did stag leaps on a diagonal, front knee bent, arms in a V. Some of the guys sprang to fabulous heights. Even Sara made it across. She didn't lift her head or open her chest, but her feet left the ground. She cracked a smile.

Afterwards, everyone clapped. The teacher took us aside and congratulated us. "I'm very impressed. It wasn't just your command of the material, it was your command over the class," she said. "It's almost as if you've been teaching for years."

By the time we locked up the sound system and stacked the mats, the change room was deserted. I squealed, "We did it!"

"Woo-hoo!" Claire stamped on the spot, pumping her arms back and forth, and I joined her. We pounded tension out the soles of our feet. "If we can make it through that, we can make it through anything," Claire said at last. "I have to get stuff from my locker. Meet you outside in five?"

"Sure."

When I left the change room, Sara was waiting in the hall. I still felt sick when I saw her, as if I'd just smashed my hockey stick into her leg. Her face looked tight, like she was holding something in. Did she want to talk about the bruise I'd given her? Maybe it hadn't healed. Maybe I'd fractured a bone. No, she couldn't have jumped across the room like that with an injury. "How's your leg?"

"It's fine."

I hesitated. "Did you like the class?"

She looked at the floor. "It was okay."

Her short replies could sure stop a conversation. I couldn't think of anything else to say. "Well, so long." I turned on my heel, but she fell into step beside me. The end of the hall beckoned, a long way off. I walked on, conscious of her keeping pace beside me.

As soon as the exit to the parking lot came into view, I said, "Have a good weekend." I pushed on the bar and walked out.

"Natalie!"

I turned around. Sara was holding the door and twisting her mouth. She seemed to be struggling for words. Watching her, I remembered how it felt to be painfully shy. The simplest interactions took colossal effort. Outgoing people had no clue.

At last, she said, "I was wondering if you might know where I could take another dance class."

I was so relieved that I almost laughed. "You scared me for a minute!"

She smiled. "It was hard to get up the nerve to ask." She joined me outside and let the door swing shut behind her. "I know I suck, but it was fun."

"You don't suck!" I said. "You did the stag leaps—I saw you. That's a pretty advanced step. And you were brave enough to cross the floor with the guys."

"It just happened that way," she said. "I waited so long to join in that the only people left were guys." She laughed. "We were all hoping that you wouldn't make us do it if we hung back long enough."

"But aren't you glad we did?"

"Yeah." She eyed the grass. "I wish I could give it another try."

"Why not?" The schoolyard was empty except for a bunch of kids waiting by the road.

She hid her face in her hands. "I can't."

I dropped my bag and pointed to a narrow strip of grass that bordered one wing of the school. "I'll do it with you. Follow me." I sprang into a series of stag leaps. The grass was the width of a swimming lane. When I finished my "lap," I turned around. Sara stood at the far end, unmoving. I walked back to her. "Okay. Let's try this again. First, let's get the arms."

I lifted my arms into a V and lowered them back down. "Join in when you're ready."

After about five solo Vs, I was ready to quit. Just then, Sara raised her arms. I slowed down to sync up with her. "Sara, that's great! Chin up. Chest wide. And up, and down. And up and down. That's it. Beautiful!"

She dropped her arms to her sides, face flushed. "I can't believe I just did that!"

"You're a natural. Do you want to try jumping now?"

"No!"

"Why not?"

"I'm embarrassed. I suck. People will see us."

"But you said you wanted to do it. Right?"

A dreamy expression flashed over her face. "Yeah."

"Then let yourself. It's okay to suck. It's okay to be embarrassed. It's okay if people see you."

She scrunched up her face.

"What's the worst that could happen?" I asked.

"I'll look like an idiot."

"Then, so will I. I'm doing it with you. I'm willing to risk it if you are. Shake on it?"

She giggled but extended her hand, and we shook. We lined up. "Ready, set, go!" I matched my height and pace to hers, and soon we moved as one. We leapt up and down the narrow strip of grass next to the school. When we landed our final jump, she grinned wide enough to show her teeth. "That's so much fun."

"I know. And let me warn you: it's addictive." Thank goodness I was taking class soon. "But you asked about classes. I think I've got a schedule in my bag."

I knelt down, unzipped my backpack, and searched the pockets. I was breathing hard from all the jumping, and satisfaction bloomed in my chest. I stood up and held out a flyer.

"Will you be teaching the class?" Sara's eyes were round and serious.

I smiled at her. "Not yet."

acknowledgments

I deeply appreciate the support of the following people and organizations: Thompson Rivers University (formerly University College of the Cariboo) gave me a two-year Writer-in-Residence position during which I completed the first draft of this novel. Thanks especially to George Johnson. Carolyn Allen, my Ph.D. dissertation advisor, needed a house-sitter when I needed a place to write. My classmates in Lisa Moore's fiction workshop, part of the University of British Columbia's Booming Ground program, were the first to hear me read aloud from the manuscript, and I'm very grateful for their positive reactions. Later on, Booming Ground's Mentorship program allowed me to rework the entire manuscript with Gayle Friesen, and she gave me invaluable guidance and encouragement. Susan Juby was an inspiration in her role as Writer-in-Residence at the Greater Victoria Public Library, and she set me back on course at a crucial stage in the process. Professional Development Funds from Thompson Rivers University, Open Learning allowed for a retreat to Hornby Island, where I completed final revisions on the book. Thanks to Alison Kooistra who, with insight and grace, made the editing process a joyful collaboration.

I would like to express heartfelt thanks, as well, to all the dance teachers and choreographers I have worked with or admired over the years. To name a few: Wendy Green, Maureen Eastick, Lynda Raino, Connie Cooke, David Earle, Lori Hamar, Hannah Wiley, Shannon Hobbs, Crystal Pite, Andrea Nann, Nicole McSkimming, Ali Denham, Joanne Winstanley. And my deepest gratitude to all the women with whom I've shared a passion for dance and who became dear friends, like Sue Lundgren McDonald, Melissa Walter, Ruth Kampen, Aletha Banner-Ennis, Lucinda Johnston Lawrence, Courtney Ryan, Christine Schieberle, and Jane Griffith. Dance is the only activity I've found that provides—all at once—a physical, artistic, social, and spiritual outlet, and I'm grateful for the communities that gather to practice and celebrate it in all its myriad forms.

about the author

JODI LUNDGREN grew up in Victoria dancing and writing. Later on, she trained and performed as a dancer while pursuing a Ph.D. in English in Seattle. The winner of a Canada Council Emerging Writer's grant, she has published one other novel, *Touched*, and her short stories and creative non-fiction have appeared in *Dropped Threads*, *Adbusters*, *Room of One's Own*, *Capilano Review*, *sub-Terrain*, and others. After two years as Writer-in-Residence at Thompson Rivers University in Kamloops, she returned to live in Victoria, where she teaches English and Creative Writing at Camosun College.